ADDISON

&

THE BOUNTY HUNTER

GALACTIC FEDERATION SERIES –
BOOK IV
THE BOUNTY HUNTER
SUB- SERIES

C. A. SALO

Addison & The Bounty Hunter

GFS 4

C. A. Salo

For my Dad.

Who tragically passed away November 2023.

He never read any of my novels, but he inquired whenever we spoke, which was regularly. 'How are your books doing, kid?'

I miss him and his unwavering love and support.

Other Works by C. A. Salo
Listed at the end.
With a sneak peek into
Space Warrior
Book V of the Galactic Federation Series
2nd book of The Bounty Hunter sub-series

CHAPTER 1

"CAPTAIN, YOU NEED TO look at this!"

Senji Ootook stopped the conversation with his second-in-command and turned to look over his shoulder at the neophyte who'd just joined his battle cruiser. Senji's brow lifted as two of his men dragged a struggling female his way. Turning fully, he noted his second-in-command and good friend Barkolth Zinnig coming forward to stand beside him, as they thrust her down to the ground. "Explain."

"Commander Alk and I saw her running through the shrubs and gave chase." Gion stated. "We weren't sure at first what it was until we caught her. I don't think she's from here sir."

Senji met Alk's gaze. He was a competent commander and good with the men.

"I thought she might be a concubine at first Captain, but then after we caught her, I couldn't find any markings of ownership. I tried talking to her. I think she hears me but can't understand what I'm saying." Alk said.

"Have you run a neuro trace?" Senji asked.

"No sir, the female balks every time we try."

Senji frowned as his gaze lowered to the female. She wasn't cowering or shaking, she just sat there, head up with eyes lowered. He could tell by looking at her that she wasn't from this planet; her hair color alone gave that away. She was humanoid but he couldn't place her point of origin. "Woman, where do you hail from?" he asked, gaze narrowing when she neither responded nor acknowledged him.

"Do you see what I mean, sir?" Alk asked.

Senji stepped forward, his boots stirring the dust on this miserable desert of a planet, and when he stopped in front of her, his brow arched as she finally lifted her gaze to his. "Where do you hail from?"

Her gaze narrowed and lips tightened to a thin line, but she didn't respond. Kneeling, he noticed that while she followed his movements closely, she didn't back up, and met his gaze when he was eye level. Which for such a small female was new to him. Men twice her size had cowered when he'd stepped near them. "What system are you from?"

Her fists clenched and he wanted to laugh. There was no way she could harm him, she was such a small bird, Senji was surprised it took two of his hunters to bring her in. "Do you understand what I'm saying to you?"

Her eyes flew over his should when Barkolth stepped forward. She was very aware of her surroundings and kept his eye on her as Barkolth spoke.

"Captain, it's highly unlikely she wouldn't have a neuro translator. It may have been damaged, thus the reason she won't speak to us. She simply can't understand what you're saying."

"Even if her translator was damaged, Bark, we'd still be able to place her planet. I don't think she's from this quadrant."

"Hell fires, she's so damn small I don't think she's from this system. I've never seen a petite female such as this, not with her physical attributes. Damn those blue eyes alone are something I haven't seen in awhile."

He raised his hand, and Senji saw that her eyes flitted, head tilting slightly to the left as he wondered whether she had been mistreated. Her focus then returned to him, and he slowed down. Tapping his ear, he then pointed her way. Tapping it again, he then said. "Can you hear me?" and motioned to his mouth, smiling when she nodded slightly.

Turning quickly with the sounds of an explosion, Senji tapped his earpiece. "What the hell's going on?"

"We caught our target," second commander Tupu breathed. "Bringing him in."

"It's about damn..." spinning when he heard Alk swearing his brows lifted as neophyte Gion grabbed the female and she came up swinging, then had him on the ground in one move. Her small fist struck him smack on the nose and barely heard the words she uttered before Alk tackled her to the ground. A medic ran up, and Senji stood by as the sedative worked and the female lay unresisting on the ground. "Want to tell me how a little bird took out one of my commanders and a newbie?" he growled as the medic repaired Gion's broken nose.

"This is why it took two of us to bring her in, Captain," Alk said. "She's small but she's spirited." He chuckled.

"And maybe I need to send the both of you through training again," he snapped, his tone bringing them to attention. "Get her to my quarters, the transcript of what she said to you, and have Diwaabas check her over. I'm done with this planet." Senji clenched his jaw as Alk lifted her unconscious body into his arms and they both took off quickly.

"You know," Barkolth smiled. "They do have a point."

"Here's my point. Why in the hell fires of Rehten is this bounty taking so damn long we had to trounce an entire village to capture him?"

CHAPTER 2

SENJI STARED AT DIWAABAS. "Are you sure?"

"Oh yes, Captain. I've ran the scan three times to make certain. She's from Cion Three, or as her people call it, Earth."

Arms crossed over his chest, Senji snorted as he shook his head. "How in the hell fires did she end up on Watu?"

"That I'm still trying to figure that out. I did a rundown through the data base and have found no missions or assignments sanctioned for that sector."

"So the Galactic Federation hasn't sent anyone in lately?"

"No sir, only for rest from duty or to swap out teams on the planet."

"Did you contact the wellness center there and talk to Jianna?"

"I did, and she has no clue how this young woman ended up here. The warriors that have gone to the wellness center have all left on their appointed times with no issues occurring during their stay. I also sent her all of our guests' information to see if she could find anything out about this female."

Senji rubbed the bridge of his nose between his forefinger and thumb. "Which means, someone's going in under the scope." Sighing, he glanced over at the Earth female sleeping on his bed. "Install a neuro translator for her and let me know when she wakes up."

"Of course, Captain."

Senji turned for the door and stopped. "Diwaabas, do me a favor and scan for trackers in her, somehow I don't think whoever took her just left her on Watu without a way to get her back."

"I'll let you know if I find anything."

Senji nodded before heading out the door and up to the bridge of his battle cruiser where Barkolth stood. "Keep the deep scans open, I have a feeling we may have company."

"Meaning?" Barkolth asked as Senji took his seat.

"Whoever nabbed her off Cion Three might come looking for her."

4

"Think they'd try?"

Senji shrugged. Anyone wanting to take on his battle cruiser would be out of their mind. The Seeker was fully manned with handpicked personnel and loaded to the hilt with Regnetron technology. "If they're stupid or desperate enough to go up against a battle cruiser full of bounty hunters. Did Gion send up the transcript of what she said to him on Watu?"

"Yes, sir. Bringing it up, now. It appears she told him, to 'get the fuck off her.'"

Senji smiled. "She's feisty for someone from Cion Three."

"I'll say so. I thought the females on Cion Three had re-emerged as passive again."

"Apparently not. We'll have to speak with Jianna more to find out how they've progressed."

"What surprised me was she didn't back down from you. She met your gaze. I don't

know of any female, even on our world who hasn't lowered their eyes at least."

"She is an enigma, Bark."

Senji brought his hand manifesto up, trying to concentrate on the newest list of bounties sent out by the Galactic Federation Council, and all he could think of was the little Earth female. After several moments he slapped it down and narrowed his gaze at the helmsman when he glanced over. Hells balls, it wasn't like he'd been long without a female, so why was his body gearing up with but a thought?

"You all right there, Cap?" Barkolth asked with a smile.

"You have the bridge," rising up his jaw clenched when he noticed Barkolth grinning. "I have something to check into."

"Don't you mean, someone?"

Senji's scowl deepened as he met Barks grin. "Yeah, so get to hunting on why the hell we have a Cion Three female on Watu. I want signature readings on plasma trails if we can find them, start with all the exporters and poachers in the Cion planet cluster."

"Cion—are you crazy? Do you know how many are listed, and those who aren't, how in the hell am I supposed to find the ship who lifted her?"

The side of Senji's mouth lifted. "By using your ultra-intelligence and smart whit. I suppose you better get started instead of staring at me like a Jack-a-poll." Strolling to the lift he grinned as the door closed. That would teach Bark from opening his big mouth in front of subordinates. Now if they'd been alone or with other officers, he would have bit back a smart reply.

"*Captain?*" Diwaabas said through their internal communication devices.

"*Yeah?*"

"*I think you best return to your quarters, the young female is awake and...*"

Senji ran at the sounds of a scuffle. "*I'm almost there.*" As he turned the corner, his door opened on its own and he slid to a halt as Diwaabas flew backward toward the wall. "Cease!" the door closed behind him as he stepped over to help Diwaabas stand, noticing the female make a run for the door. "It will not open for you, and you are no longer on Watu." She turned and met Senji's gaze, her back to the door, her eyes wide and her chest quivering. "We mean you no harm, a neuro translator has been installed so you should understand what I'm saying now." His eyes lowered to her chest and noticed her heartbeat slowing down slightly. "Do you know who took you and dumped you on Watu?"

"Maybe it would be best if we start with formalities instead of questioning techniques." Diwaabas said. "My dear, my name is Diwaabas, and I am the head medic on board. This is Captain Senji Ootook, and you are?"

"Addy, Addison Harper." She said softly.

"Addy, Addison Harper, the translator is working properly for you then?"

"Yes, and it's just Addison, Addy is a short version of my name."

Senji kept his gaze on her as she spoke with Diwaabas, She was soft spoken and damn if his cock didn't take notice of the girl. Maybe it wasn't such a bright idea to have her in his quarters. "Addison, can you tell us how you ended up on Watu?"

Her crystal blue gaze flew to his. "They left me. I think they were being chased."

"How long ago?"

Addy's gaze lowered for a moment then rose. "I want to say two weeks."

"I don't know what your week is."

"Um, fourteen days. The sun rose on Watu like it does on Earth, so fourteen sun risings or the moons came up thirteen times."

Senji nodded his head then tapped his earpiece. "Bark, the female says who took her was being chased, that's why they dumped her and fled."

"Time Frame?" Bark asked.

"About thirteen moons. Check the Federations records for anything that matches."

"On it." Bark replied.

Senji noticed the female was more relaxed now. "Can you tell us how you were taken and when?"

"Are you the police or something? I mean you look like a cop, but well, maybe military?"

"I do not understand the words police and cop. I am not military."

"I think she wishes to know what we do, who we are." Diwaabas said.

"We are bounty hunters sanctioned with the Galactic Federation."

"Bounty hunters." Addy said.

Senji smiled as her brows lifted and gaze moved over him. "Yes. We were hunting a fugitive on Watu. That's why we were there. Can you tell me anything about the ones who took you?"

"I really didn't get a good look at them. They snuck up behind me and by then it was too late my vision started blurring. They kept me heavily sedated until they dumped me off." Her gaze slanted down. "I remember they were guttural-sounding."

"Guttural?"

"The language they spoke-it was, harsh, clipped, where yours is not."

"Captain, if I may, why don't we have Yolami sync with her?" Diwaabas asked.

"Good idea, then we'd know for sure. Yes, com her please."

"Ah, who is Yolami and what is a sync?" Addy asked.

"Yolami is one of the telepaths we have on board." Senji replied. "She will be able to mind sync with you and go deep to seek the answers we're looking for."

"Not sure if I'm liking that."

Senji caught the slight fidget and quickening of her heartbeat. "You will not be harmed, and she will not go where she should not."

"Will it help catch my kidnappers?"

"Yes."

"Are there any side effects?"

"Fatigue and you may start remembering the events more clearly."

CHAPTER 3

SENJI'S GAZE STAYED ON Addison as Yolami synced with her.

"She is walking, the moon is coming out, she's calm, slightly stressed about her job and the ass who's her boss." Yolami snorted. "Don't blame her, what a dick."

Senji's brows drew together. "Yolami."

"I'll fill you in later. She's sensing something, frightened, she knows someone is following her, faster. Ahh, awful smell, like rotten meat...'

Senji's gaze widened as he met Diwaabas'.

"Arm grabbed, something over nose and mouth, turning. *Oh* yes, she sees them right before she goes under. It's the Suknan's."

"Those bastards." Diwaabas grumbled.

"Stay with it Yolami, I'm curious what happened until we locate her." Senji ordered.

Yolami nodded. "Yes sir. Very hazy, they drugged her, small glimpses. They took samples of blood. She tried telling them to stop, pain. *Oh*, oh, shit, they cut her, different places, different depths to see how her body reacted. A needle near her eye, oh damn! The pain, by the Gods. They took some fluid. Crying, scared, screaming, but nothing's coming out, sharp pain on shoulder, red dust, hot, she's on Watu. Scared, drugs have worn off, she's forging for food, finds a small water hole. Stays away and hidden, scared, explosions, loud noises, they see her, running, fighting, she's fighting with Alk and Gion. Oh, what a punch to the head," Yolami chuckled. "She nailed Gion in the privates, anxiety, can't understand what they're saying, heartbeat quickens, she's looking up, oh, she meets your gaze, Captain. She's not afraid, anxiety, but, intrigued, huge, ooohh, private thoughts, she senses you're not going to hurt her. Hand, jerks, sorry she made you feel like you were going to hit her. She likes how you tie your hair back and have the underneath shaved and your tattoos. Ooooo, um, private thoughts. Explosion, adrenaline sky high, jumps and hits Gion, gut reaction,

9

oomph, Alk body slammed her, sore, wants to cry, ooh pinch, everything, going black."

"Did they bother her womb?" Senji asked, glimpsing Diwaabas turn to him.

"No they didn't get that far."

He exhaled loudly, his eyes closing for a moment. "Thank you, Yolami. You can disconnect." Stepping forward, he knelt by Addison, as Yolami ended the mind sync. Her eyelids fluttered and shiny blue eyes met his. "How are you feeling?"

"Um, okay, weird." Addison said, rubbing the side of her head.

"You'll be fine," Yolami said as she leaned forward with a smile. "The residual effects will go away shortly. If you take a nap, you'll wake up and everything will be back to normal."

"I'm not sure if I know what normal is anymore."

"Would you like to go lie down?" Senji asked.

"Yes please."

He lifted her and stepped into his sleeping quarters with Diwaabas behind him. "I have to return to the bridge, sleep and rest. If you're hungry when I return, we'll get you something to eat."

"Ok, thank you."

Senji nodded as he brought the cover up and over her. "One of my warriors will be outside the door should you need them. It will open for you now. All you have to do is walk up to it." His gaze on her as she nodded, her eyelids flittering closed and when her breathing evened out, he turned to Diwaabas. "What?"

"Do you ask for her or you?"

His gaze narrowed.

"Just asking." Hands lifted palms out to show his subordinance. "I shall take my leave and head back to medical."

Senji growled as he left, his gaze turned to the little Earthling. Shit, he knew his actions were something his crew was not used to seeing from him. He was relieved the Suknan's had not touched Addison's womb. That was Diwaabas' department, not his. And Yolami...damn, he knew when she mentioned private thoughts. Addison was attracted to him, having the same feelings he obviously had for her. What the hell was that about? He'd taken plenty of lovers, had never experienced his body's reactions over a female, except this little Earthling. Heading to the door, he nodded his head at the warrior standing outside his door and reached out via internal communication to Bark. *"The Suknan's grabbed her. They had her for maybe a day before they dropped her on Watu."*

"Those grimy bastards, figures. I'll run the comparisons for their ships and update the federation."

"Sounds like a plan, I'm heading to the bridge."

"Meet you there."

Senji stood in the lift, stepping out onto the bridge the same time Bark did.

"How bad did they hurt her?"

Senji sighed. Everyone knew of the Suknan's penchant for experimenting on their captives with no pain blockers. "They withdrew blood and cut her. The cuts we thought were from the bushes on Watu were from the Suknan. Thankfully, they didn't have her long enough to do any real harm."

"The Gods were watching over her. I heard from Jianna, Addison was reported missing by her employer, she has no family, her last relative passed on several years ago."

"That's why they grabbed her." Senji sat on his chair as Bark went to his station. "Progress on finding the ship?"

"We've narrowed down three, I will have the signature matches before shift end and Reff is running the diagnostic on the tracker Diwaabas extracted from her shoulder. It's still active. Once we have the information there, we'll be able to pinpoint which ship she was on."

Senji nodded and lifted his hand manifesto. "We have four hours before we enter the Eridana Galaxy. Make sure the team is in the command room in three. We hit Agimisus in four and half."

"Already done. Alk has coordinates on the bounty."

"Let's not have another Watu."

"I'll do my best, Captain."

Senji glanced over to see his grin. "Make sure you do. You wouldn't want to chase another plasma stream across the galaxy." His mouth titled up when Bark lost his smile. That would teach him, the smart ass. Moving his gaze back to the manifesto, he scanned who was in the sector and smiled.

"Who do you get to hit?"

"What?" Senji asked.

"You're smiling."

"Ha, you think you know me so well." Meeting Bark's gaze. "I'm not going to hit anyone. Our favorite Retriever team is in the sector."

"No shit, Mella and the girls are in Eridana?"

"It looks that way. Why don't you issue a greeting for them to come on board after we have our bounty?"

"Damn, man. I'm already on it."

Senji chuckled. "You do remember hearing they all took mates, right?"

Bark looked up and Senji laughed. "Damn it."

"And from what I hear, Janeska has a babe."

"I knew I should have approached one of them. Good women like that don't stay single for long."

"No, they don't. Have no worries, Bark. When you find your mate, you'll know it."

"Yeah, one of these days. Ok, we have the diagnostic in on the tracker and..."

Senji waited as Bark's hands ran over his console.

"We have the ship. It's a Suknan cruiser. They're in the Galavian Cluster."

"Send a missive to the Federation, for a warrant."

"Working on that now."

Senji nodded before he rose. "I'm heading to bio and then my quarters; I'll meet you in command for the debrief."

"Yes, sir."

CHAPTER 4

ADDY STRETCHED, A MOAN escaping her lips as her hands went above her head. She didn't know why, but she felt safe for the first time since she'd been taken. Maybe it was because the Captain had been so gentle with her, he hadn't hurt her and neither had his crew. Her arms flopped on the bed as she stared at the ceiling. They reminded her of mercenaries, they were all large, muscled and tattooed up. But the Captain, Senji, damn, she liked that name and him. He was not a pretty boy-you could tell he was a warrior through and through. Rugged, hard lines, five o'clock shadow and his long black hair drawn back Viking style on the top, shaved on both sides and tied at the nape of his neck. His hair had to be below his shoulder blades and his tattoos, he had them everywhere, not on his face, but the shaved portions of his head and his arms. Damn, her body shivered.

"Are you all right?"

Her Kegels clenched with his deep voice. "Yes. I mean, I think so. Am I supposed to remember what she was able to see?"

"Yes. Yolami only synced with you. The items she seen and spoke of will show themselves easier to you now."

Addy gripped the covers as she remembered. Damn, she'd much rather daydream about him, a single tear slipped from the corner of her eye as she turned to meet his gaze. "They cut me," She whispered. "Everywhere, I could feel my blood running from the wounds." Sitting up when he sat down, she entered his arms, and held on to him. Her nostrils flared, chest heaving as she tried to calm the fear within.

"They'll never hurt you again, Addison."

She closed her eyes. "Why would they do that to me?"

"The Suknan are a horrid race, they care nothing for the pain they inflict upon others."

Her breathing slowed, his heartbeat under her ear and caresses from his hand soothed her. "What are you going to do with me?"

Senji leaned back and met her gaze. "What do you mean?"

"If I go home, no one will believe me. They'll probably stick me in a psych ward and drug me up and if they do believe me, I'll probably end up in a government facility being experimented on."

"The Galactic Federation has strict guidelines on entities taken from young worlds. Cion Three or Earth as you know it, is considered a young world, although it is seven million years old. Its life forms, humans, as you call yourselves, have been inhabiting Cion Three for about five hundred thousand years."

Addy shood her head. "That's impossible. The human race isn't that old. The first form of human evolution is only about two-hundred thousand years old. I mean, we didn't even start becoming civilized until about six thousand years ago." His grin had her Kegels clenching.

"You have much to learn. But to answer your question, I have several options. I can turn you over to the Galactic Federation, and they will help situate you onto a world of your choice. You can become an ambassador of Cion Three, but that will take years before they allow you to return to the planet and they will force you to change your looks from the bone structure in your facial features to the blood flowing through you. Or you can stay with me."

Her breath caught. "Stay with you, how?"

"I can take you as a companion, and as such you'll be allowed to travel with me when I'm out hunting."

Her brows drew together. "Companion, you mean like friends or friends with benefits?"

"I do not understand your analogy."

"Ah," she met his brown gaze. "Friends like, let's go grab a drink or friends like, glancing down, as her hand stoked the comforter.

Senji chuckled. "Ah, I understand. This is what Earthling's call being intimate, benefits?"

"Well only on a certain level. It means, sleeping together but not invested in a relationship." Addy lifted her gaze when his fingers nudged her chin up.

"A companion on my world is treated with respect. We are with one another and no one else. While you will not have the status as a mate, the taking of a companion is a way for us to become familiar with one another and if we at some point feel, we are not matched. Then we go our own way, and I would of course help situate you with the Federation." Senji said as he kept her gaze.

"Oh, have you ever taken a companion before?"

"Once, when I was younger, before I became a bounty hunter. You?"

"Yes, once. It didn't end very well."

"Explain."

"He didn't like that I wanted to walk away. He hit me, once, and ran like hell. Why are you smiling?"

"I have seen you take down one of my newly trained men and toss Diwaabas. He was right to run, and I am glad you defend yourself when needed."

Her gaze lowered with a soft smile and lifted when his fingers threaded through her hair, his thumb caressed her jaw.

"I am attracted to you Addison, as you are to me. As you are from Cion Three, I am aware you do not show mating signs. How do you know when you sign with your mate?"

"I, I don't know. Is that something that happens with you?"

"Yes."

"Oh, what, what signs do you have?"

He grinned. "We can start the change."

Her brows furrowed. "Change? What kind of a change?"

"Males of my world will bulk up, we become larger. Sometimes our eyes will glow." His head tilted when her eyes widened.

"Become larger? Holy crap, you're huge as it is. I mean, I'm lucky if I come to your armpit and you're strong. I mean damn, look at these muscles."

Senji chuckled when she squeezed his bicep. "My world Gruna is a world of warriors. We do not wear masks like other bounty hunters or extractors, as our people are known for no mercy if someone dares attack us." He liked how she moved her hand over his arm. She was not afraid of him. "Addison." He grinned when she kept caressing him. "Addison."

"Hmmm?"

His nostrils flared when her scent released. She was sexually excited. "I want to kiss you." He met her gaze when she lifted her head. "I don't want to scare you. You've been through a lot."

Addison smiled, her hand laying on his forearm. "I'm okay. You're huge yes, but you've been very gentle with me. I, I feel safe with you Senji."

When she leaned in he let her take her time as she touched her lips to his. Her small hands lay on his chest as she sat up on her knees and leaned down. This time he met her, his hand on her hip as he kissed her back. Damn, she had soft lips. His tongue lined her bottom lip before delving inside her warmth, groaning when she met him, he moved her to straddle his lap, and drew her closer.

Addy sighed as he took over, his lips and teeth moved down her neck. Tilting her head, she groaned when they landed on the spot between her shoulder and neck. Her hands gripped his shoulders, loving how his muscles moved beneath her fingertips.

Senji ground his cock against her heat, and Addison moaned, rubbing her mound against him harder. When the chime went off, he groaned, hugging her to him as he lay his head on her shoulder. She trembled when his hot breath hit her neck.

"Why...why are we stopping?"

"Because I have to be in the command room in thirty minutes for a mission."

"Oh."

He lifted his head and met her passionate gaze, his cock twitched, and her lips parted. "Sorry."

Addy smiled. "Me too. I can honestly say, I've never had such a reaction to a man."

Senji grinned. "Good to know, my little one. You have an effect on me as well."

"No, I, I never kiss on the first date, and we haven't even had a date."

"I am honored." Lifting her off his lap, Addison met his quick kiss before he hopped up. "I need to gear up. After the mission, we have some friends coming on board for dinner and drinks. You'll like them. They're all female and the best Retriever team in the Federation."

"What is a Retriever team?"

Addison liked how Senji answered her questions as he went about dressing, and when his last weapon was placed, he turned to see her quietly watching him.

"What's wrong?"

"Nothing, besides the fact that, damn! You make me horny just looking at you. Just, be ok, okay."

Addy smiled when Senji stepped over and knelt down in front of her. She couldn't believe she'd told him that.

"No worries, we prepare well, and our clothing is made on Du'Shara, a warrior world, best gear out there." He nuzzled her hand when she cupped the side of his face.

"I have never felt like this with or for a man before, so be safe out there."

"I shall, my little one." Leaning in his lips touched hers softly, glad when she reacted to him and held her lips or a moment before backing off. "I shall. I'll send Yolami to show you how our showers and clothing centers work. I'll be back before the evening meal."

"I'll hold you to that sir." And smiled as he rose and headed out the door. Damn the man was just too handsome. She loved warriors, not sure why, but she'd always had a thing for them. And when she met his gaze that first time, something in her lightened up.

CHAPTER 5

Senji stepped over a log, heading to the coordinates with Granger and toward their capture. Agimisus was a wet world with moss hanging from the trees and poisonous creatures everywhere. Good place for a man to run if he was smart enough to cover his tracks.

Senji growled as he stepped over to their bounty. "You have made me late for an appointment."

"Fuck you!"

Tupu chuckled. "Wrong thing to say, man."

Senji picked him up by his shirt and met his gaze, as his feet dangled and eyes widened. "You're wanted for trafficking stolen goods among other items. Be glad I don't kill you outright Erald." Letting go, he turned as Alk grabbed the fugitive up. "Let's go!"

Senji stepped into quiet quarters and headed to the shower unit. "Computer, where's Addison?"

'Addison Harper is in the officer's dining area with your other guests.'

"And Bark?"

'Commanding Officer Barkolth, is in the officer's dining area.'

Senji grinned as he stripped. "I bet he is." *'Bark.'*

"Captain?"

"I'm showering up and will be there shortly, how's everything going?"

"Noted and great. Addison is getting along extremely well with the ladies, they are at this moment chuckling and Soma is warning her about warriors from Gruna and their sexual appetites.'

"Shit, she better not scare Addison off."

'She's laughing and saying something very softly about liking a passionate partner. So, you're thinking about taking her as companion?'

"I am, thoughts?"

"I like her. She has a good personality; we know she can defend herself and she's not afraid of you.' He chuckled. 'Has either of you shown any mating signs?'

Senji reached for a pair of pants. *"As far as I know, Cion Three is still too young to exhibit any."*

"And you?"

"Yeah." He glanced into the mirror; his eyes glowed briefly. *"I'm on my way."* Stepping out into the hallway, he made his way to the officer's dining area and listened as Tupu said, "Captain in the room," shooting him a look. "How the hell did you beat me here?"

"I'm quick, sir."

"Senji! You hot piece of male, how are you?" Soma said.

Senji smiled as Addison turned with a smile of her own. "I'm great Soma, how are you and your new mate?" embracing her as soon as she approached.

"Oh, we're good. He doesn't like it when I leave, but when I get back, damn, I'm surprised I'm not pregnant yet." She laughed.

He chuckled as she backed up. "Zedan's a good male. I hear he made the ambassador of Pli skulk away at a council meeting."

"He sure as hell did. Damn, I love that man."

Senji moved to Addison, his hand going to her lower back. "How are you feeling?"

"I'm well, thank you."

He smiled as he kept her gaze, glancing up when he heard chuckling, to see Mella smiling. "What Janeska?"

"You, Ootook. I never thought I'd see the day."

"Mmm, how's being a mom treating you?"

"Oh great, he's just like his father. Bossy and impatient."

Senji chuckled. "Well, he is a prince of dragons."

"Yes, I've had to douse Draven several times. But damn, it's fun having a mate." She chuckled.

"She's a mermaid." Addison said. "Or that's what we call her kind on Earth."

His fingers caressed her back. "Yes, I've heard of the term." He smiled at her. "And how is Captain Mella doing?"

"I'm fine Senji. I heard you had a run in with Korth."

Senji met her gaze. "I did. He's a sly one."

"He is that. And, yes. What you're being shown is true." She smiled.

"Really now?"

"Yeah."

"So how's the Admiral?"

"He's great, on a black op right now."

"How are you three doing with not being on a ship all the time?"

"It's weird." Soma stated.

"Yeah, but we know we can go out." Janeska said.

"Being on a planet all the time is, boring." Mella rolled her eyes.

Senji chuckled as his chef called for the meal to being. "Ladies, please." He guided Addison over to the chair to his right and arched a brow when Mella grinned.

*

Addison smiled as Senji walked her back to his quarters. "I like them."

"They are something, huh."

"Are all your friends like them?"

"Yes, my close ones."

She waited until he glanced down at her. "What did Mella mean when she said, what you're being shown is true?"

"My signs."

She glanced down for a moment before meeting his gaze again. "Your mating signs."

"Yes."

Addy let him lead her into his quarters outer chamber before she turned to look at him. "Are you seeing them?"

"I am."

Her head tilted; he was difficult to read. A good trait for a bounty hunter. "Are you okay with that?" Her eyes widened when his shimmered.

Senji shrugged. "I wasn't expecting it, but if this is what the Gods want, I'm good. We're both attracted to one another, and we seem to get along."

"Did you see these signs, before or after that kiss in the bedroom?"

"Both."

Her brow lifted and Kegels clenched when he kept her gaze. "I like that." Her chest lifted, nipples brushing against her bra, and noticed his hard-on when he lowered his gaze to her breasts. "You don't think it's too early, do you?"

"To early for what?"

"Us wanting to have sex. I mean, we don't really know each other that well."

"We can wait if you wish, but I warn you now, it will be more aggressive."

"Oh." Breathlessly she met his gaze again. "I'm not understanding why, when we're alone, my body goes crazy. Lust is one thing, but this, I've never experienced. Do your signs somehow affect me?"

"They shouldn't, but not a lot is known of your kind mating to mine."

Tingles ran from the back of her head down her spine, her lips parted with an indrawn breath. "Senji."

"I will try to be gentle my little one, but..."

"I'm good with it." Stepping up, she wrapped one hand around his waist and the other up his back, her mouth lifting as his lowered and moaned, his tongue breached her and she met him. Shivers of pleasure ran rampant over her heated body. He growled as she took his mouth possessively, the kiss turning to an aggressive mating of mouths.

He lifted her to him, carrying her to his bed, her body trembling as he lowered her away from his heat. His hands gently cupped either side of her face, tilting her head just a bit to fit her perfectly. She opened to him, and his tongue swirled inside.

Addy moaned, her hands lifted to lay on his chest. One kiss and he had her body soaring; if this wasn't a sign she didn't know what was.

His tongue thrust deeply, his scent and taste flooded her senses, her Kegels contracted, and essence slipped out to wet her thigh. Damn, she'd never been this wet in her life, her sent her spiraling and she melted against him giving him permission to do anything and everything to her. Breathing heavily, she met his gaze as he stripped, and she lifted the flowing material of the dress, Yolami had said was of their people. Her hands shook and she moved them away as he took over.

Senji filled his palm with a full, firm breast. His thumb ran over her turgid nipple, his roughness as he teased had her arching her back toward him. his dominance as he ground against her heat, she spread her thighs wider, rubbing her clit against him, moaning with need. Lowering a hand between her legs, his fingers slid easily between her labia, brushing a finger over her nub as he pinched a nipple. Damn she was wet, so wet for him. Senji moved, grabbed pillows and shoved them under her lower back. Slipping back into place, her thighs widened for him, his nostrils flared with the scent of her excitement and his cock jumped. He gripped her hips with his huge hands and entered her slowly, his bulbous head disappearing between her sweetness. He lifted his gaze, her eyes were closed, lips parted as he moved an inch.

"Senji, please, more." She gasped, her legs wrapped around his thighs, her pelvis arching.

"Nay, sweet. You're so tight, I don't want to hurt you."

"You won't, please."

He leaned forward, pushing himself in a fraction more as he crashed his lips to hers. She opened under him with no hesitation, her hands roamed his impressive chest and shook with urgency, as he moved into her more, and tweaked her nipple with his fingers. "Damn, you're so small, my sweet one."

"You feel so good. Shit Senji, you feel so good."

Withdrawing, he nuzzled the side of her neck as he entered her again. He'd never been so exhilarated being inside a female. "You do as well, my sweet." Withdrawing, he entered her slowly again, until he sat fully inside her. Closing his eyes, with a groan, he bit her neck, his body trembled when hers did. "Fuck, baby. You feel good." His hot breath hit her sensitive skin.

Shivers ran from one end of her to the other. "Oh God."

"Are you all right?"

"Oh, yes, oh, don't move." With one little shift, he bumped her womb and she fell apart. Crying out with her climax, her pussy tightened around his thickness, her body jerked. Feet solid on the bed, she pushed against him, his cock moved, and she cried his name.

Senji leaned forward, kissing her chin as her eyes opened, glaze and unfocused. "You're beautiful."

"Oh, don't move. It hurt a little."

Senji lowered his hand to her pelvic and started caressing her muscles. "That's it, relax your muscles for me, sweet one."

"I, I'm sorry, that's never happened to me before."

CHAPTER 6

SENJI SMILED, HIS MOUTH meeting hers. "Never be sorry for the pleasure we share." He groaned and kissed her softly, his hands and mouth moving over her. When she started responding, he withdrew and thrust in, flexing his hips in quick short thrusts. His teeth sank into the place between her shoulder and neck and after a few more thrusts, he quickened his rhythm, every plunge bringing them closer. He'd never been like this with a female, never had the urge to have one so completely. His blood screamed for her.

Sweat pooled between her breasts as she thrust up to meet him. Her lips parted with gasps and moans. "Please, please, again, deep, I like it deep." Close, she was so close. Her gaze widened as his eyes glowed and his cock thickened, Addy's eyes rolled back. "Ohohohohoo, Senji!"

He moved his hands up her back to hold her shoulders as he plunged into her with fierce thrusts. When he breached deeply again, she shattered, her body jolted against him as she cried out his name. His fingers gripped the back of her head as he roared with his release, his hips bucking before he collapsed on top of her.

Addy moved shaky hands up his forearm to his bicep, his muscles moved under her caress. "Wow."

"Are you all right?"

Smiling when he lifted his head. "I'm fine." Cupping the side of his face, she lifted, kissing him softly. "Oh." She chuckled when his hardness twitched inside her.

"He wants to play again. Are you sore?"

Addy moved her hips. "A little, but it's a good sore."

Senji groaned as he withdrew from her slowly. "Then we stop."

Addy gasped at the feeling of losing him. "Senji, no, please." Reaching for him, she grabbed his arms, halting him. "Please, we don't have to do anything more, please, just, stay inside me."

Senji returned, his leg moving up, so he could lie beside her. He moved most of his weight off her. His gaze narrowed at the sigh of contentment floating from her passion-swollen lips. Laying his head next to hers, he wrapped his arm around her. He knew what was happening with her; it was a sign of his people. A sign that said she was his mate, along with his glowing eyes and thickening cock right before her orgasm. He knew he wanted to take her for a companion; what he hadn't counted on was taking a mate. And until he did, she'd want him like this after every mating. Moving his gaze, he noticed her breathing had evened out and he drew the covers up over them.

*

Addison sat on the sofa, after Yolami had left. Senji had sent her this morning to answer any questions she may have had and now she had more. Rising up, she walked to the door, her gaze following it as it slid silently to the left and looked up meeting the guards. "Hi, um, do you know where Senji is?"

"Most likely on the bridge."

"Oh, do you know if he's busy?"

"He's always busy, ma'am. He's the Captain."

"Oh, right. Do you know if I'm allowed to do anything besides sit in here all day?"

"I do not know."

Her brows drew together. "You're not helping very much."

"Apologies."

"Well, I thought you were here in case I needed something?"

"Are you in need?"

"Of information I guess, but you don't know if Senji is busy, what's his friend, Bark doing?"

"Commanding Officer Barkolth is on the bridge as well."

"Oh. Do you know if I'm allowed on the bridge?"

"I have no orders that say you are not. But unless the captain brings you there himself or you are cleared, visitors are not allowed."

He was starting to piss her off. "Well then, have I been cleared?"

"Not to my knowledge."

"What orders do you have?"

"To stand guard at the captain's quarters and assist you."

Her hand fisted and lips thinned. "Are you being obstinate on purpose?"

"Ma'am?"

"Don't you ma'am me, you know exactly what I'm saying and you're pissing me off." Raising her fist to him, she stomped her foot and turned, knowing the door shut as she went to the bedroom and flopped on the bed.

*

When Senji stepped into his quarters, her gaze moved with him as he went to the bedroom.

"Are you ready for dinner?"

"What I'm ready for is a damn good fight." Crossing her arms over her chest when he stepped in between the two rooms.

"Explain."

"Explain, my ass." She ground out through clenched teeth. "Didn't your guard out there fill you in?"

His brow rose as he moved to stand in front of her. "He mentioned you wanted to come to the bridge and that I and Bark were busy."

"Ha!" flopping back against the sofa, she moved her gaze to the ceiling, her nostrils flared with deep breaths. "I've been sitting here all-day stewing. I was trying to find out if I was allowed to do anything but sit here all day. I asked if you were busy, he said most likely, I asked if Bark was busy, he replied the same. I asked if I was allowed to do anything, he replied he didn't have orders on that." Meeting his gaze. "Am I allowed to do anything besides sit here all day? I will go crazy with boredom..." Senji cut her off when he picked her up and lowered his mouth to hers.

Addy groaned, her flaying hands landed on his shoulders, drawing him to her. After several moments, she moved her hand up to the back of his head and gripped his braided hair, until he broke the kiss. "Ok, not mad anymore."

"No?" he grinned.

"Uh-huh." Sighing as his mouth moved to her neck.

"Are you hungry now?"

"Mmm, but not for food."

Senji chuckled. "I also, my sweet one. It was hell staying away from you today."

"Then why did you?" she asked leaning back to meet his gaze.

"You were sore after last night and when you didn't stir when I rose for my shift I figured you needed the rest."

Addy curled into his caress as his hand cupped her cheek, his thumb running over her lips.

"Did Yolami answer your questions?"

"Yes, but I had more, that's why I wanted to see you."

"Did she have you get into the med unit?"

"No," she shook her head. "I didn't want to do that." His head tilted and he frowned.

"I don't understand, why would you not want to be healed?"

"It's not that I don't want to be healed, it's just that, well, I didn't want to take away the sensations, as slight as they were, that I had from our love-making."

Senji smiled as he nuzzled his nose to hers. "I understand." And chuckled when her stomach growled. "Come, let us feed this hunger first."

Addy chuckled when he grabbed her hand, bringing her behind him and out the door.

CHAPTER 7

SENJI BEHAVED HIMSELF THROUGH dinner, but the moment they were alone in the corridor to his quarters, he lifted her to him, attacking her mouth hungrily.

Addy brought her arms around his neck and legs wrapped his waist, hugging him to her as her tongue plunged into this mouth. When he set her on the bed, she jumped up and shoved him back. His surprised look had her chuckling as she lifted and removed the dress. Going to stand between his open thighs, she ran her hand over his uniform jacket and unbuttoned it quickly as he did his pants, and she moved to straddle him.

"Addison." His hands went to her hips, gripping.

Taking his bottom lip between her teeth, she bit down and lowered herself slowly onto his thickness. Her lips parted with a gasp, head titled back, eyes closed as she thrust her chest to him, her hard nipples rubbing against him.

His fingers grabbed her nipples and she gasped as her pussy contracted around him, drawing out a groan. She reached up and wrapped her hand around the back of his head, grabbing his hair, and came down on him.

Drawing a nipple into his mouth, he grabbed her hips, making sure she didn't come down too hard. She liked it deep; it was up to him to make sure she didn't overdo it, for too many hard thrusts to her cervix would bring her pain, not pleasure.

Her pace became quicker, her head spun as tingles swarmed and ran down her spine. Her eyes opened when his fingers threaded into her hair to the back of her head, her lips parted as she met his gaze.

"You will wait until I give you leave." He ground out, plunging inside her. When she started drawing in deep breaths and holding them before releasing them, he growled and surged into her. "Now, my sweet, release for me."

Addy's eyes rolled back with her cry of ecstasy, her insides convulsed on him, and she could feel his release inside her with his groan. Her chest heaved as she collapsed against him.

Senji drew her into his embrace, his hands caressing her back, her tremors had him moving back on the bed and drawing the covers over them as she lay on his chest.

"What do you do to me?"

He chuckled, kissing the side of her head. "I could say the same, my sweet. I have never initiated a mating in the corridors."

Addy lifted her head, blowing hair out of the way so she could see him. "Captain, I fear we may have a problem."

"Oh yeah, what's that?"

Her Kegels clenched with his smile as he moved his arms up, interlocking his fingers behind his head. "You'll need to come here for lunch so we can ravage each other and get it out so we can take our time after your shift."

"By lunch, I'm assuming you mean the mid-day meal."

"I am."

"It will depend on the day and what is happening."

"Ok, but we have to find something for me to do while you're working. I don't like being bored."

"Then we will go over tomorrow what attributes you have and where you may be needed."

"Yay!" Clapping her hands, she sat up and moaned as his thickness moved with her.

Senji chuckled as he lifted her off him. "What other questions did you have?"

Addy sat on his thighs. "Well, I asked Yolami want it meant when your eyes glowed and your...." she motioned to his cock. "thickens."

"And she told you they are signs we are with our mate."

Addy nodded. "Yes. I remember you saying something along those lines." Her head tilted and she paused. "But well, I mean, what do you think of that happening?" She lowered her eyes.

Senji moved his arms, cupping her face between his hands and waited until she met his gaze. "The Gods gave us the gift of the signs to know our true mate is with us. Was I expecting it, no. Did I have an inkling? In all honesty, yes. Just meeting your gaze on Watu, I knew there was something about you."

Leaning forward she lay her hands on his chest, her lips touching his softly. "So, you're okay with it?"

"Yes, are you?"

"I, yes." She smiled. "Although I would have liked us to get to know each other better, but dang, it's hard to describe what you do to me. Are you okay with me being from Earth? I don't have any special abilities, like Mella and them."

Senji chuckled. "You do have a special talent, my sweet. You are the only female to have me hard all day just by thought of you."

"Really?" her gaze wide, then the corners of her mouth lifted. "I like that." Laughing when he growled, he rolled her to her back as he attacked her mouth.

'Captain to the bridge, Captain to the bridge.'

Senji groaned at the automated voice of his ships internal systems. "Why?"

'Not known, Captain. Commander Barkloth has requested your presence.'

"Bark, what the fuck?"

"Sorry, but the Suknan cruiser is headed right toward us."

"Fine." Glancing down he met her gaze. "I have to go my sweet, Bark needs me on the bridge."

"Is everything all right?" her eyes narrowed when he stayed silent. "Does it have to do with me?"

"Are you a telepath?"

"No, but I'm pretty good at ready body language and whatever he said to you on your internal link you're not sharing." Her brows rose when he glanced over his shoulder meeting her gaze.

"I do not want you to worry."

"Whether I worry or not, Senji, I don't want you keeping things from me."

"The Suknan ship that grabbed you, is headed our way."

"What?" she jumped up. "Oh God, what are we going to do, I mean, will they..."

Senji grabbed her by the arms. "Addison, they will not get close to you, do you hear me?"

"But they're, they're coming. Senji, they're coming."

He drew her to him, holding her tight until she calmed slightly. "My sweet, I will never let them hurt you, do you trust me?"

"Yes." She hadn't hesitated. "I trust you."

Senji nodded. "Get dressed, you'll come with me."

Her mind swirled as she grabbed her dress, her gaze flittered to him as he dressed and took his hand, silently following him.

"Captain on the bridge."

Addy looked over at the man who announced Senji, her gaze going to Bark as his brows lifted. But he knew not to question his Captain in front of others.

"Bark, in my office." Senji ordered.

Addy followed him to a room off to the side and sat where he put her, behind his desk, as the door opened silently, and Bark stepped in.

"I assume by her heightened heartbeat, you told her?" Bark asked.

"I did." Senji answered.

"No worries, Addy. They won't even get close." He snorted.

"Update, Bark. You pulled me away from being in bed with her.

Addy gasped. "Senji, don't tell him that."

"I'm sure he knows that's where we were."

"I did," Bark answered. "As the tracker remained active, and we haven't moved in a few days. The Suknan ship set out two hours ago on a direct course to us. Of course, they probably have no idea who we are. Your orders, Captain?"

"I don't want them near the ship. Is there a safe planet close to us, where we can lay a trap?"

"There are several. Cekirius is our best option. Little life signs, in case of a fight, and enough cover to hide us from them until we want them to know we're there."

Addy's gaze never left Senji and as he nodded his head, she noticed a change about him, he was all business. Not the carefree lover she'd just snuggled up to in bed. Her ears perked when they mentioned one of the female hunters onboard would pretend to be her and met Senji's hard gaze when he turned to her.

"Would you mind us taking a sample of your hair?"

"No." she answered softly. He had that hardness to his eyes like when she first met him, although she couldn't blame him. He was a bounty hunter and had to be on top of his game to ensure his crew and his safety was not compromised.

"I've also received the warrant from the Federation for the ships capture. We are a go." Bark said.

"A warrant?" Addy asked as they both turned to look at her. "So, what they did to me wasn't allowed?"

"No." Senji said as he turned. "What they did is against the Federation's code. We do not take inhabitants of worlds, especially young ones, to do what they did. They were in violation the moment they entered the Cion planet cluster. It's off limits to those like the Suknan."

"They've done this before then?"

"Yes, unfortunately, too many times. They are about to have all their ships restricted to their planet's orbit. The Federation is growing tired of their abuse of cultures.

Her gaze lowered for a moment. "Senji, you don't have to bring them on board, do you?"

"No, my little one. They will be confined to their ship."

Glancing up when he knelt in front of her, she smiled softly. "Okay."

"Okay," he smiled. "Let's get you back to bed, shall we?"

Addy nodded and took his hand.

CHAPTER 8

ADDY GLANCED OVER AT Senji several times during dinner. He was sharp and to the point with his officers, even Bark, and that she didn't like. Usually, he was not as formal. Slowly lifting her drink. Something was up. Lifting her gaze, she glanced around. They knew something and they didn't want her to know. "All right." Setting her glass down, it clinked in the odd silence surrounding the table. "What the hell is going on?"

"Sweet?" Senji asked.

"Don't you *sweet* me. Something is up. I may not be a telepath or a warrior with internal links, but I'm not an idiot either. Not only are you guys communicating with your internal links, so I don't hear you, you—." She said and met Senji's gaze. "Are hiding something from me and I don't like it."

His gaze narrowed and she held it, narrowed her own and tilted her head, then widened her eyes. "Do not play games with me Senji Ootook." Lifting her finger, she pointed at him.

"Are you sure she's not a telepath?" Tupu asked.

She never wavered from Senji's gaze. "No, Tupu, I'm just fucking smart."

Senji's gaze widened as Bark chuckled. "You my sweet, swear too much."

"Then I wouldn't suggest really pissing me off, I have no holds bar when I'm ranting." Her brows lifted as he grinned. "Now, you tell me right now, what's going on."

"Not sure if that's a good idea."

"Does it have to do with a mission?"

"No."

"Does it have to do with the safety of this ship or her crew?"

"Not exactly."

"Then you had best come clean, Captain, or you'll be in the doghouse tonight." His brows arched as Diwabass chuckled.

"Well, fill the rest of us in." Bark growled.

"He'll be sleeping on the sofa with no mating."

The corner of her mouth lifted, and eyes narrowed as Senji's brow lifted.

"Really?" Senji asked.

"Try me." Thankful her tone came out as confident as she had hoped.

Senji sighed. "Fine. Cekirius, is refusing to let us use the planet for the trap, as we have no reason to be on the planet and no bounty to take in. which leaves us two options."

"They are?"

"We hide the ship behind the farthest planet moon in case there is a fire fight when they see our ship, or ..."

"Or what?"

"We place you on the planet with the tracker and use you as bait."

"Hmmm." Her gaze lowered.

"You're too quiet. What's running through that head of yours?"

"*Star Trek* episodes."

"Star what?"

"What's more dangerous for the crew?"

"Ship on ship fight. Although we have more fire power and defense, they could always get a lucky shot in."

Addy's chest lifted with a long indrawn breath. "Okay then, I go down to the planet."

"No!"

Her gaze whipped back up to his. Her head tilted as they stared at each other. "Senji?"

"I will not have you in danger. You are my mate, we will think of something else."

Addy smiled softly as she glanced at the others around the table who had wide eyes. "Um, not sure you wanted to mention that, that way."

"I announce our mating publicly. I have been shown the mating signs by the Gods and take Addison Harper of Cion Three as my mate." Senji stated. "Any problems with that?"

Addy lowered her head and grinned when they all said, 'no.' she didn't really think they'd speak out against him, especially if they knew of the signs. "Senji, stop being so matter of fact and bullying." Lifting her gaze, she met his. "I have a plan."

*

"I'm still not liking it." Senji grumbled.

"Sshh." Addy whispered, laying her hand on his forearm as they hid in the forest; their 'bait' sat on a rock about five-hundred feet from them. While she had to be on the planet as she was the Suknan's target, and they had a bounty on the Suknan ship and crew, she didn't have to be in the midst of danger. That and the fact she geared up like one of his crew is the only reason Senji agreed to her plan. He'd still complained but said she looked too damn hot, and she better not leave his side. The corner of her mouth lifted at his reaction when she'd stepped out of their bedroom behind Yolami, who had done her hair very similar to his after she'd helped her into clothing from Du'Shara and some weapons. Apparently, the clothing would protect her if she was shot, unless it was from a thermal canon and several others. She didn't see that happening and told him how empowered and sexy she felt. His cock had hardened immediately, and he told Yolami to leave as he guided her to the nearest wall for a quick and passionate love session.

Her gaze lifted when Tupu motioned with his hand and leaned to glance past Senji as three men came out of the forest toward Feleia. The female was similar to her body size, as she wore her clothing from Watu and they were able to make her hair as red as Addy's, from taking a sample and simulating it. Her fingers clenched and Senji's other hand came up to cover her hand as the Suknan jumped Feleia. When she turned with a weapon aimed at them, the other members of the team's crew including Tupu and Bark ran out, covering them.

She waited until Senji moved forward and met the gaze of the Suknan as Bark read the warrant against them. Her fist balled up and she stepped forward, punching the closet one right on his so-called nose. Her lips lifted with a snarl as she made contact with her left fist, the pain jolting her hand not as exhilarating as the scrunching sound of the impact and brought her right fist up again. Her chest heaved as he flew back, nostrils flared as she took a step toward him and watched him cower.

"Get up, you bitch," she snapped. "You want to kidnap me and cause me pain, try it while I'm not drugged." Her gaze narrowed when she noticed the team back up out of the corner of her eye. Stepping up, she kicked him hard. "Get up!" She grasped his collar, the rasp of material tearing in her ear. Her fist hit him again, greenish blood spattered, his head lolled, and she tossed him to the ground standing above him. Shaking her hand, she snorted before turning to Senji. "He's all yours." She lowered her gaze and stepped over to sit on a rock, her back to the others. Her stomach turned and hands shook as the adrenaline left. Damn, she hadn't meant to go off like that, but it had felt so good.

"I told you not to leave my side."

"Yeah, sorry, I'll suck your cock to make it up to you." Her voice waivered and she glanced over at his chuckle.

"You will suck my cock, because you want to, not because you have to."

A small smile lined her lips as she met his gaze. "I'm sorry Senji."

"Mmm, let me see your hands and tell me where you learned how to fight."

Addy winced as he pressed on her knuckles. "Ah, I um, I took some classes, for defense at first, then I liked being able to punch my anger out on the bags."

"Well, I will say the Suknan deserve everything you dished out, and I think you scared Bark."

"No I didn't," she chuckled. "He doesn't seem the type to scare that easily." Glancing up at movement out of the corner of her eye to see Bark and Tupu leading their captives.

"I am not pissing you off." Bark grinned as he walked by.

"You wouldn't happen to have a sister, would you? I like a challenge." Tupu smiled, wiggling his eyebrows.

"Welcome to the family, my sister." Feleia grinned as she shoved Tupu from behind.

Addy lowered her gaze and cleared her throat, lifting her eyes when Senji's fingers tilted her chin up.

"My crew approves of my mate. Now come."

Addy took the hand he held out and let him help her rise.

"We have the second part of the mission which needs to be completed. Do as I ask this time, Addison, and go with Gion back to the Seeker. I will see you there shortly."

She met his kiss, her hand laying on his chest. "Be safe."

"For you, and go see Diwaabas to have your hands checked out."

"I will." Stepping back her gaze followed him as he caught up with Bark.

"Ma'am."

Addy turned to see Gion standing to the side of her. "Yes, I know, to the ship and to see Diwaabas."

"Yes ma'am. And may I say, thank you for not unleashing on Alk and me like you did on that Suknan, when we found you on Watu."

Addy chuckled. "I wasn't mad on Watu, I was scared." Following in step next to him, she grabbed his arm when the transport started.

Her stomach clenched and now she knew why McCoy never liked the transport.

CHAPTER 9

SENJI STEPPED INTO HIS quarters and was met with silence. His brow furrowed and headed to the sleeping chamber; the corner of his mouth lifted when he noticed her sleeping on the bed. Diwaabas reported to him that she had small fractures on both hands, which he healed in the med unit and Gion reiterated her dislike of the transport. Removing his gear, he stored it quietly and drew his shirt over his head as he went to the sonic shower. Stepping in, he sighed as the warm rays removed the dirt and grime from his body, his head lowered, braid falling to the side as small hands moved on his back. "I thought you were sleeping."

"I was."

"Diwaabas' report stated you had several knuckles with fractures."

"That dweeb, he had to tell, didn't he?"

Senji chuckled as her naked body moved against his from behind. "Of course he did, I'm the Captain, everything that happens on this ship, I know about."

Addy slipped in front of him. "Are you tired?"

"A bit why?"

"Can we have dinner here tonight, you know, just the two of us?"

"We can, after my shift." He leaned down, lips brushing against hers. Her breathing was even and adrenaline levels normal. "If you're up to it, we can go down to bio and see if we can find something for you to do while on board. Although, I'd like to keep you away from danger."

"Hmm, what happens when a man from your planet mates with a female and they're both warriors? Does she get to stay being a warrior if she wants? Like if Tupu and Feleia mated?"

He grinned. "You, my sweet, are very observant, and to answer your question, if two warriors' mate, it's up to them to make that decision. Gruna males are very protective over their mates. I've seen where and we have a few mated couples on board who have compromised, the

44

female still keeps her status, but will go to a non-fighting team. While we are all bounty hunters on this ship, and there's always that chance even someone like Yolami may have to step up if the ship is under attack, and fight. She is in a non-violent position on board, while her mate keeps his position on a retrieval team."

"Oh, Yolami is mated?"

"She is." Leaning over to turn off the shower, he stepped out with her. "Commander Brol, the man who stands to the left of Bark is our head security officer."

"Oh, I think I saw him when you brought me up there."

"He was there." Grabbing a pair of pants out of his clothing center, he smiled as she asked to go back to the bridge. "For what reason?"

"Because it was neat, and I want to see it better."

Senji turned as he drew a shirt over his head and met her gaze. "Because it is neat," he chuckled, "is not a reason to bring you to the bridge."

"What about you tossing me on your desk and ravaging me? In every position." she smiled.

His lip curled with a snarl. "Woman, if I'm hard for the rest of my shift, I will spank your ass."

"I might like it."

He groaned as she giggled and walked to the bedroom after her, his hand coming down with a smack on her ass cheek.

"*Oh*! Senji!"

He chuckled. "You asked for it my sweet, now get dressed and we'll go to bio."

*

Addy glanced at the warrior in front of her, clapping her hands. "Well, what does it say?" Senji had left her with Tumos before going to the bridge. They were heading to a Federation holding station for the bounties they had on board and in tow.

"Um, well." He scratched his head. "I've never seen more than one position come up before."

"Oh, like what?"

"You said you worked with the public, right?"

"Yes, retail, I hated it, but it was a job." She sat up. Her eyes widened when he glanced up at her. "Ok, well come on, stop keeping me in suspense."

"The read-out says you would be good as a Chef's assistant, a researcher or an ambassador for your race."

"Wow, that's so awesome! I like cooking and planning parties, and I love to research stuff. Not sure about an ambassador though, they have to be all political and everything and my mouth tends to get me in trouble." Her brows drew together, and the side of her lip lifted. "Maybe I should do the research thing, because with Senji as a Captain, I'm sure we'll have to host parties if someone important comes on board and everything." She grinned as she met his gaze.

"Would you not be happier helping the Chef?"

Addy frowned. "Why, what's wrong with me wanting to be a researcher?"

"Well ma'am, to be a researcher you have to have knowledge of our systems on board and the galaxies around us, never mind the means to..."

"Are you saying I'm not smart enough to learn?"

"No, I'm saying at this point as you are new and from a young world, you may not be able to integrate with our technologies and..."

Addy stood, nostrils flaring. "Are you calling me stupid and ignorant?"

"Ma'am..."

"You ass." Storming out she headed to the lift. "Bridge!"

'You do not have access to the bridge, Addison Ootook.'

"Stupid computer. Bring me to Senji!" Her arms crossed over her chest she waited until the door opened to see the bridge and the crew turn to see who was in the lift. "I'm not on the bridge!" She met Senji's gaze. "Your dweeb down there is a jerk and called me stupid." Stomping her foot, her chest heaved as the lift doors closed. "Bring me to Yolami." Tingles swamped her, her nose pricked, and eyes teared up. No one had ever called her dumb in so little words.

"How in the hell did she get the lift to bring her to the bridge with no clearance?" Bark asked.

"She obviously is not stupid." Senji stated.

"And that was the second time she was able to solve issues that none of us had considered. She has a talent there Captain." Brol said.

*

Senji turned when the door to his quarters swished open to see her walking in. "I thought you wanted to have dinner here?"

"I do. I was mad and upset." Her shoulders slumped. "I went to see Yolami, and she introduced me to your practice chamber or gym, so I could hit the bag for a while."

He knew where she had been. The moment she left the bridge he'd located her with the computer. Glad she was comfortable enough with another female to seek her out. He didn't like seeing her defeated and moved to her, his hands settling on her shoulders and waited until she lifted her head to meet his gaze. "You my sweet are neither stupid nor ignorant."

"I know. I just-it's not nice to hear someone belittle you like that."

"He has been reprimanded."

She shrugged a shoulder as the corner of her lip went to toward her mouth. "It doesn't matter."

Senji lifted her, went to the sofa, and sat down with her on his lap. "It does matter. From what I understand, you are multi-talented. I have never seen more than one reading come up on anyone, and sweet, I've been doing this for a long time." When she curled into him, he wrapped his arm around her.

"Maybe I'll just stay here and be naked for you when you come in."

"While that is a fantastic idea, my sweet, you will be bored within days and I'd rather have you happy." His brows lifted when she sat up.

"Hey, now that we're mates, what happens if I get pregnant?"

"Well, that's a switch if I ever heard one, but to answer you, we have several options. You can either stay on Gruna at my dwelling or you and the babe can stay on ship with me."

Her brows drew together. "What if I don't want to get pregnant right away? I mean we haven't had a lot of time for us, and a baby is a lot of work. And well, I want to be selfish and not share you for a bit."

Senji smiled. "While a child with you would be a joy, I too would like time for us. We can go see Diwaabas."

"Okay." She jumped up.

Senji rose taking her hand. "Now, back to the other topic." And grinned when she sighed.

"Do we have to?"

"Yes, now, I hear you would like to be on the research team." He turned as they stepped into the lift.

"I thought I'd like to try it."

"Excellent, you have a meeting with Lieutenant Gartas in the morning after roll call," he smiled when she glanced up. "And my sweet, she's excited to meet you."

"Really?"

His brow lifted. "Did I not say so?"

Addy smiled as she jumped on him, kissing him as he chuckled and wrapped his arms around her.

CHAPTER 10

ADDY SMILED AS SHE moved over his lap, straddling him as they sat on the sofa.

"What are you about?"

"Did you eat enough?"

"I did, and you?"

"I did. But I want a sweet later." She smiled as she ran her hand over his chest. She liked the uniforms when they weren't geared up, it was like a t-shirt and camo pants, but all one color, and theirs was a dark grey.

"You may have whatever you wish, my little one."

"Tell me why you say *my* before words when referring to me."

"When we are with our companions or mates it is a form of endearment. You are mine as I am yours."

"But you used it before you even asked me to be your companion or showed signs as mates." She met his gaze and loved how the golden flecks swam in his brown eyes.

"I did. Somewhere deep down, I knew you were to be mine."

"You make me melt." Moving her hand up, she traced the tattoo on the side of his head. "What does this mean?"

"It's the symbol of my family."

"Tell me of them."

"I am the second son. My brother will take my father's seat as head of the family when he passes or becomes incapable of leading."

"Does he have a family?"

"He is due to mate with his companion this coming birthing season."

Addy kissed the side of his head before leaning down to meet his gaze. "You don't sound happy about that."

"It's not my business, and I told him so, along with she was not suitable for him."

Her brows furrowed. "How would you know that?"

"She attempted to mate with me while being with him."

"Did you tell him that?"

"No."

"Holy crap, Senji, that's one thing I'd want my friends or family to tell me. Trust me, I've been through it."

"I don't want to..."

"Hurt him, I know, but she hit on you while being with your brother. There's something wrong with her. He didn't sign, did he? Is she from Gruna?"

"No, they have not signed, and no she is not."

"Okay, off them, you have a mom and dad, any sisters?"

"Yes, two younger. Evasia is an Operations Officer on board the Parthian, it's a battle cruiser with our space fleet, and Miki is more at home on planet being a lady of my parents dwelling."

"Interesting." Addy murmured, lifting the hem of his shirt, he sat forward enough for her to remove it. "What's this one?"

"My Captain rank."

"Oh." She placed her lips on it, then trailed her finger down the line of hair on his chest to the edge of his pants. His muscles moved beneath, and his dick twitched against her warmth.

"Addison?"

Her fingers spread as they moved back up his chest to lay over his peck. "I want to take my time with you."

"You're making me horny."

The sides of her mouth lifted as she met his gaze. "I'm making myself horny." Gripping his pectoral muscle, she leaned over taking his nipple into her mouth.

"Damn sweet."

She smiled as his head leaned back to rest on the sofa, her lips and teeth traveling up the side of his neck. She stopped and nipped right under his ear, before taking his lobe in her mouth. "I like how you love me. You're aggressive but gentle, and you know when to go deep enough to send me over the edge."

"My little one, you are about to send me over the edge."

"Mmm." Placing her hand on the other side of his throat, she caressed his jaw with her thumb, her mouth covering his, before leaning back to take his bottom lip between her teeth and sucked it into her mouth.

His hands moved to her hips, and she grabbed them, bringing them up behind his head. "If you touch me, I'll let you do whatever you want to me."

Senji chuckled. "I like that." She groaned as she rubbed her breasts against his chest.

Addy giggled as she slid down him, her fingers releasing the front of his pants. "I believe I promised you something on planet." Her tongue ran along her bottom lip and fingers shook as she reached–jumping with a screech when an alarm sounded and the computer said something about a breech. She yipped as she was grabbed, to see Senji holding her.

"Come with me."

"Bark?"

"Intruder on your deck heading right to you, we're on our way."

Addy went with him as he headed to the bedroom and started gearing up. "Senji?"

"We have an intruder heading right to us."

Her gaze wide when he turned. "What do we do?" He slapped a weapon in her hand.

"Use it if you have to."

Addy shrieked with the sound of an explosion, her hands covering her ears as the ringing in them brought her to her knees. Her eyes squinted as debris flew past the door and Senji headed that way. Crawling to the door, she could barely see as he fought two men, then a blast of light flew him back off his feet. "Senji!"

A shuddering breath left her as she lifted her weapon and fired, taking one man out as the other headed to her and she fired again, missing him. She cried out as pain ricocheted through her hand. Coming up with her other fist, she knocked the man away as she crawled to Senji who was coming to his knees.

Addy cried out as her hair was grabbed, meeting Senji's gaze as she was lifted.

"I have what is yours, now find what is mine."

"Let her go, Korth!"

Addy squirmed to break loose. "Let me go!" Turning, she lifted her fist, hitting him on the neck, but he just laughed.

"Woo, you have a live one here, Senji."

"You fucker! Let, me go!" Her hair yanked as she turned again, punching him right in the balls. When his hold loosened, she jumped away, but not fast enough, and she cried out.

Senji rushed forward, tackling them both.

Addy oomphed, scrambling out of the way as the men fought and jumped-up grabbing a piece of the ship that had been blown in, smacking the other man on the head as he tried to get up. Turning as the men tossed blows at one another. Eyes wide at the blood dripping down Senji's side, but that didn't stop him.

"Well this has been fun Senji, but I really must go." Korth said as he backed up and nodded.

Addy caught on to late as she was grabbed, her gaze wide, and met Senji's as her stomach flipped. Coming out of the transport, she went to all fours, dry heaving.

"Somehow I don't think you're one for transporting. So, you're Senji's mate. You're definitely not from Gruna."

"She's awfully small, and all that red hair. Where are you from, baby?" another male voice asked.

Her fist clenched as she glanced up, eyes narrowed through tendrils of hair. "You, hurt, my, Senji." Her tone low, she came up quickly, her right fist connecting with the side of the man's head. Straddling him, she hit him again. "I am not your baby!" glancing up when chuckling perked her ears, she advanced on the man named Korth. "You bring me back to my mate!"

"Not until he finds what is mine."

Her nostrils flared, fist hitting her thigh. "If you lost something, that's your fault." She snapped, her gaze going to the man getting off the floor. "You back off or I'll put you right back down there." Whipping her gaze to Korth who was almost the same size as Senji. "Did Senji take what you're looking for?"

"No."

"Then why are you doing this?"

"Because he has the means to find it."

"Does he even know what *it*, is?" she spat as his gaze narrowed.

"Yes, and it will do you well not to piss me off, woman."

"It will do you well not to piss me off, asshole. Because I'm warning you right now, if you don't send me back, I will make every living moment with me, hell."

CHAPTER 11

"SIR, YOU NEED TO SIT still so I can heal you." Diwaabas said.

"Activate the tracker, I want her found now!"

"We're on it, Captain." Bark said.

Senji's gaze narrowed as Bark stood in front of him. "How the hell did they get on my ship?"

"We're still trying to figure that out."

"If he harms her..."

"Senji, Korth does not want you hunting him down. He won't harm her, he knows it will get him nowhere."

His nostrils flared as he punched the exam table he was sitting on. "I want her back Bark and I don't care who we have to kill to do it."

"What's he looking for?"

Senji met his gaze. "His mate."

"What?"

"Korth has a mate. Her brother found out and ripped her from him, hiding her."

"Who the hell did he sign with?"

"Come with me." Rising, he headed to his office, not saying a word until he brought up a secure channel. "This is Senji Ootook, I need to speak with King Zeldar now, it's concerning Korth."

"King Zeldar on Nagarr?"

"Yes." Senji replied, his gaze going to Nakoss when he came on vid.

"Senji, what's going on?"

"Korth invaded my ship and took my mate. He will not return her until I bring back what was taken from him."

"By the Gods, he's a menace."

"I'm going after him now, but so help me Nakoss, you need to give her back."

"I will not!"

"He took my mate, because you took his!"

"Senji, I apologize, but she is my sister, and I must protect her."

His fist came down on the consol. "If it was your mate he took, I doubt you would answer the same."

"You are most likely correct..."

"Captain, we have them." Tupu stated over the com.

Senji's gaze never wavered. "We will speak more after I have her back." Nakoss nodded before the screen went black. Turning he headed back to the bridge. "Where is she?"

"The ship has been located in the Theta star system." Tupu answered.

"Engage the cloak, I want every team on this ship ready for a fight. Bark, Tupu, meet me in the command room with the Commanders in thirty. We're going dark."

"Yes, sir."

Turning, he stepped into the lift and headed to his quarters. Walking by the clean-up teams, he headed to the bedchamber. He didn't gear up in his bounty hunter uniform; he had his leather Grunanian breastplate which fit over his head. He tied the sides and glanced up, seeing his bare tattooed arms and weapons. His jaw clenched and eyes glowed. Turning from the mirror, he headed to the command room.

*

Addy rolled to her side with a cringe. She knew she'd hurt her hand in the fight, but she'd be damned if she asked for anything from this asshole. But her hand was swelling, and she needed it to cause havoc. Going to the door, she met the guards gaze when it opened. "I need the med unit."

When he motioned for her to come out, she did as he commed Korth. The ship wasn't as big as Senji's and when she stepped into the med unit, he was already there. She was silent as his doctor scanned her hand, stating she had multiple fractures and healed her with a handheld device.

"Is she pregnant?"

Addy met his gaze. "No, I am not."

"She's correct sir, she is not carrying." The doctor replied.

"Where are you from?" Korth asked.

"Does it really matter?" she snorted.

"She is from Cion Three." The doctor replied.

Addy shot him a look as he backed away.

"Cion Three, impossible, I thought the females were back to their passive stage."

"Then you thought wrong, dumb ass."

Korth chuckled. "Where in the fires of Rethen did Senji find you?"

"On Watu where the Suknan dumped me."

"Suknan, damn darling, they had you. How bad did they hurt you?"

His concern surprised her. "What does it matter to you? You are no better than they are. You took me from my home for your own selfish reasons and hurt me."

"I mean no harm to you."

"Well, what do you think you're doing? You took me away from Senji, you hurt me when you blew through our door, and you hurt him. He was just trying to protect me."

Korth's head went down. "He knows where to find my mate."

"Your mate? What are you talking about?"

"My mate was taken from me by her brother, Senji knows him well and has been a source of negotiation between us. Her brother has hidden her away from me."

"Why? I mean, did you hurt her?"

"No! I would never harm her. He took her because of who I am, what I do. I know he was trying to protect her, but he has no idea how ripping her from me has hurt the both of us."

"Tell me." She said softly.

"She is a dragon shifter from Nagarr, I have feline abilities. When we signed and became mates, we connected on a more, primal level."

"I do not have abilities, but I know what you mean. I've never connected with anyone like I have with Senji. I don't have mating signs, but I know he was meant to be mine. Even after what the Suknan did to me, I trusted him. I didn't know why at first and I was very jittery, but he, he calmed me, calmed my fears and all he had to do was hold me."

Addy whipped her head around when someone ran in.

"Sir, the Seeker is coming in hot, she's cloaked, we picked up on the plasma trail, and she's not slowing down."

"Well, my dear," Korth said as he stood. "It seems Senji is not playing."

"Please," she whispered. "Please give me back, so no one gets hurt. I will talk to him about your mate. I will do all I can to help you, but please no more fighting."

Korth sighed. "Very well then. I did not mean to cause you harm and I would never want anyone to go through what I am."

Addy patted his hand and met his gaze as he stood. "I will help you."

"I know the transporter makes you ill, but it's the quickest way for me to get you back to him."

"I'll stomach it." She smiled and let him lead her to the transport room.

"Computer, open a channel to the Seeker."

'Channel open, sir.'

"Seeker, this is Korth. Stop and de-cloak and I will return her."

Addy gasped when she heard Senji. "This is Captain Ootook. This better not be a trick Korth."

"I assure you Senji, she is unharmed and wanting to return to you."

"Shields are down."

Addy took Korth's hand and stepped on to the pad as he did. Gripping it as they transported, the next thing she saw was Senji and a team standing in front of her and smiled as she met Senji's gaze.

"Let her go." He snarled.

Addy released Korth's hand and stepped forward. Senji was not in his normal gear, and damn, he looked bigger than life as he stepped forward.

"Are you all right?"

"Yes, yes I'm fine, but you, you were bleeding."

"It's nothing."

When he grabbed her arm, she jerked back. "No, I know what you're thinking. You let him go back."

"Do not argue with me on this, Addison."

"Do not tell me what to do Senji." Lifting her finger, she pointed at him. "You knew his mate had been taken, didn't you?" Her gaze narrowed when his did. "Don't you narrow your eyes at me, Senji Ootook. His mate was ripped from him."

"He is with the Hela Crime Organization."

"I don't care if he's the devil himself." She poked his shoulder. "They had no right, brother or not, no right to rip her away from her mate."

"We will speak of this later."

"Oh we will, all right, you can damn well guarantee that, mister." Poking him again, she narrowed her gaze when he did. "Now you let him transport back with that stomach stirrer, because I'm tired."

"He has warrants on his head."

Addy sighed loudly. "And I am back where I belong with no bloodshed." Her gaze lowered as her shoulders slumped. "I'm tired, Senji," she whispered. "I just want to be held by you." She glanced up when his hand cupped her face.

"Send him back to his ship. Korth, we do *not*, want to meet again."

Korth saluted him with a smile as he disappeared.

Addy curled up to him when Senji brought her into his embrace, her arm wrapping around his neck as he lifted her into his arms.

CHAPTER 12

SENJI STOOD BY HER side as Diwaabas checked her out.

"I'm telling you I'm fine. He did not hurt me and healed my hands when I asked from me hurting them when they attacked and brought me back to their ship. I'm more worried about you, you were bleeding."

"I am fine. Now let him check you."

"Senji..."

"You will not argue with me on this." He snapped as he met her gaze and she lowered hers. When he glanced up Diwaabas moved his gaze from him back to his task.

"She's fine, Captain. You may take her to your quarters."

When Senji set her down on the bed he met her gaze. "Are you well?"

"I told you I was tired. I told you I was fine, why did you not believe me?"

"I wanted to make sure."

"I am so mad at you right now. You snapped at me for no reason, and I've been through a lot today, you know." Her eyes glistened with unshed tears.

Senji knelt in front of her. "I did not mean to snap at you. I've been worried for you. I was scared for you." Cupping her cheek.

"But I'm okay, I told you I was okay."

"You don't understand who Korth is little one. He has killed many at the whisper of a word."

"I know he is a man who is going through the same things you just told me about."

"Why do you defend him when he attacked us and took you from me?"

"Yes, he did, and I made sure to point that out in a not so nice way, after I smacked his man around a bit for hurting you."

"You did, huh?" he smiled.

"Yes, I did. He hurt you, my Senji."

His head tilted as he met her gaze. It was the first time she had used the endearment and she did it naturally.

"What is it? What's wrong?"

"Nothing my little one, everything is well." Leaning in he brushed his lips along hers. "How about we find our sleep?

"All right, but you'll have to promise to wear again what you have on now."

"Why's that?" he chuckled as he undressed her.

"Because you're a fucking hot bad ass and it's turning me on."

He caressed her breast. "Mmm, and you, my sweet, are simply beautiful. Now to bed with you."

"Join me."

"I must go to the bridge."

"No, I want you to lay next to me, please Senji."

Senji stood and drew off his breast plate. *"Bark, I'm staying with her in my quarters."*

"Aye, Captain."

Removing his pants, he crawled up next to her, drawing her close as she turned and cuddled into him. Lowering his arm, he set his hand on her hip as his leg went between hers. Her fingers caressed his chest.

"I love you, my Senji."

Senji smiled, his nose nuzzling the side of her face. "As I love you, my Addison."

*

Senji growled as he hit the wall, his fist going through it. "She was all cuddly last night, now she's a demanding, irritating female."

"Not taking her side Senji, but she does have a point." Bark said, holding up his hands as he backed up. "Come on man, not that I like it either, but what King Zeldar did was wrong. As you personally found out."

"So I've told him."

"Maybe you should let Addison have a go at him. She's pretty good at getting people to do what she wants. Hell, she got Korth to let her go within three hours of taking her."

Senji met his gaze. "You might be onto something there. Get someone in here to fix this hole, and get Nakoss on vid. I'll go get her."

*

"I don't have to do anything. Are you listening to me you, big hulk?" Addy said as Senji shoved her through the door and noticed a male on vid.

"You will tell him what you went through." Senji said.

"I won't do anything." She puffed up. "And who the hell are you, anyway?"

"Senji, who is this mouthy female?"

"Mouthy?" she turned to Senji. "Who is this asshole?"

"He's the one who took Korth's mate." Senji smiled as her eyes narrowed, and she turned to Nakoss.

"All right you..."

"I am a King of Nagarr, how dare you..."

"I don't give a rat's ass who the fuck you are, you sit back, jerkoff, and shut your mouth!" Her chest heaved. "Do you know the havoc you have caused because your selfish ass and egotistical attitude got in the way? Well, let me fill you in. You caused my Senji to take a blast and make him bleed. We were being intimate, and a damn explosion blew our door in. Then he worried about me because I was taken, because of *your* actions. Do you have a mate?" When he remained silent, her brows arched. "Do you have a mate!"

"No."

"Well, when you do, I'll be sure to make her aware of your actions." Leaning on the desk, she kept his gaze. "You have unnecessarily put others in danger because of your wants. When the mating signs hit you, and they will hit you, hard, you better think about those you've impacted, because when your mate leaves you, your guts will feel like they're being ripped out. And I'll make sure she stays away so you know the impact you've caused to me, my Senji, Korth, and your sister." When he opened his mouth, she lifted her hand, cutting him down. "I don't give a shit who he is or what he's done. You had no right. You better remember my words, King jerkoff, because I have a long memory and I hit hard." Swiping her hand across the console, she watched as the lights on the vid went down. She turned to her mate. "Okay, I forgive you." She jumped on him, and he chuckled.

"You do, huh?"

"Yes." When he sat her on his desk and stood between her legs, she opened them wide, smiling up at him as she ran her hand up his chest. "Captain, I do believe we have unfinished business." Her fingers moved quickly, releasing him from his constraints, fingers wrapped around his thickness, jerking up, loving his groan.

His lips suddenly met hers as he squeezed her ass, his huge hands moved her thighs around his hips, raising her and thrusted into her warmth as he dragged her down onto him. His tongue commanded her, her moans had his cock thickening inside her.

Addy pulled back, her eyelids heavy, lips parted. "How do you do that?" she breathed.

"It happens with my passion for you, sweet."

"Oh, God, I love it, love you."

His mouth back on hers, tangling, invading, loving, capturing her gasps, he thrust into her, sheathing himself to the hilt, her cry the sound of unbridled desire. He moved his hand, fingers finding her nub.

Her hands roved over him, gripping his shoulders, nails biting into his flesh. Her shrieks of pleasure rose, her muscles contracted. "Sen, Senji, I'm going to..."

"Release with me." When he buried himself in her deeply two more times, she shattered around him, crying out as her body jerked.

Thrusting, he touched her womb, lightning flashed down his spine, balls tightened, and with a groan he gave way to the strongest orgasm he had ever had.

Her legs flopped like dead weight as he embraced her, the side of his head rested against hers, their chests rising rapidly, he couldn't separate from her, didn't want to. Her body jerked with aftershocks, his hot breath hitting the sensitive skin of her neck as he kissed her there.

His hands caressed her back. "My sweet one, are you all right?"

"Oh yes." Addy drew back. "Oh shit, they didn't, no one heard us, did they?"

Senji chuckled. "No, my rooms are soundproof due to the delicate nature of what we do."

They both glanced to the door when a chime went off. Moving to his chair, he sat quickly, moving her dress around her.

"Senji, let me up."

"Sit still, they'll never know."

Addy gasped as his cock moved inside her. "Ohhh, not too sure about that."

"Shhh." Clearing his throat. "Enter."

She lay her head on his shoulder, eyes on the door as Bark came in and stopped when he saw them. "What do you want, Commander?"

"Ah, I, Captain, we have a missive coming in from the Federation." Senji nodded. "Send it here."

"Yes, sir."

Addy glanced up when Senji started laughing. "What?"

"I think you shocked the shit out of him, love."

"Oh gosh," she moaned, his thickness moving inside her when he leaned forward to his console.

"I know, sweet. I don't want to separate from you either, but I have work I must see to."

Addy noticed the change of his facial features as he read whatever had come in, his eyes narrowed, and jaw tensed. "Senji."

"Hmmm."

She lifted off him, his concentration on the work at hand. Straightening her dress, she glanced up to see him staring at his vid screen. "Senji."

"Yeah?"

Her brows drew together. She knew he had work and it was important, but damn it she didn't like him ignoring her when she spoke to him. Going down on her knees, she sucked his semi-hardness into her mouth.

"Frak baby."

Addy smiled as she cleaned her essence off him. "Do I have your attention now?" she asked as she looked up and met his gaze. Lowering her hand to his thickness, she stroked him. "I cleaned your cock off so you can slip him back into your pants." She removed her hand as his gaze glazed with lust. "After your shift, you will find me waiting in your office in our quarters, bent over your desk, naked, waiting for you, Captain." Leaning down, she brushed her lips across his. "Don't be late." She whispered before backing up, tossed him a smile and headed out of his office to the lift, grinning at Bark as she strode by and heard Brol say he was glad he hadn't pissed her off.

CHAPTER 13

SENJI TURNED TOWARD THE door as Addy walked through it into their quarters. "How was research?"

"Great! Lieutenant Gartas is a wealth of knowledge and knows how to train."

He loved how her eyes shone with excitement, his brows furrowed. "What, what's the matter?"

"Who did your hair?" he asked as he stepped up and around her. It had been done in the warrior fashion, much like his.

"Oh, Yolami, she asked if I'd like it up, and I said yes to keep it out of my way."

"I like it down." Moving to the front he met her gaze.

Addy lifted her hand to her head. "But it took so long to do. You, you don't like it?"

He hated seeing uncertainty in her beautiful eyes and brought her to him, his lips brushing hers. "It's fine, when we're on a mission, but I have more pleasure when it's down, running my fingers through and gripping onto it during our matings." His hot breath hit her cheek, her hands ran over his back.

"Damn it Senji, you're making me horny."

"As you do to me everyday, my sweet. Now let us go to dinner and so you know we are on our way home." Lifting her hand, his lips brushed her knuckles as he met her gaze. "I have a lot to teach you."

"Oh yeah, like what and will when you wear your hair down for me to yank and tug?"

Senji grinned as they stepped into the lift. "When we are on Gruna, I wear my hair down."

"Oh, so going home is a good thing?"

"For several reasons."

"But not for others?"

His brows drew together, as they stepped off the lift. "You are too smart, my little one."

Addy chuckled. "I've heard that before. Is it because you don't wish to face your brother and his she demon?"

"I didn't think you told her about Ekene?" Bark said as they entered the officers dining area.

"I did not," Senji growled. "But you just confirmed what she assumed."

Addy smacked his bicep. "I don't assume, assuming makes asses out of people. I read what people say and do, I read what they don't say. I can't help it, it just happens."

"A valuable trait, my sweet." Brushing his lips to hers, he drew out her chair and watched as she sat.

"She would make a good ambassador." Tupu stated as he sat.

"No," Addy said. "I hate politics and having to say things a certain way, I'd have more people pissed off at me and then Senji would have to beat them all up for getting mouthy with me."

Senji chuckled. "Oh I would, would I?"

"Of course. I can't smack them around all by myself." She smiled.

He shook his head as dinner was placed in front of them. "As you say, my sweet."

*

Addy's gaze widened as they walked out of the shuttle. His world was stunning.

"Addison?"

"It's beautiful." She whispered as she met his gaze. "So lush and green, and colorful." Her head moved to take in the flurry of colors from the flowers and trees.

"It makes me happy you see it as so."

Addy smiled, laying her hand on top of his, when he presented it to her. Her hair blew around with the breeze as they walked to his parents' home. Senji had filled her in on their culture, it was pretty much like Earth, but you were allowed to stand up for yourself and call someone out if they did you wrong. Mates were inseparable and if someone dared attack their family, they would be dealt with swiftly. He also stated his home was close, but not close enough to have his family over all the time. She liked that and the fact she could go on ship with him when he went hunting. Apparently, his team would go out every three months and come home for three unless they received an emergency transmission from the Federation.

"Why are your hands sweating?"

"I'm nervous. I'm about to meet your family, you know." Glancing up at him, she grinned at his smile, giggling when he drew her to him, his mouth landing on hers.

"Arrr, my brother has the worst timing."

Senji laughed and Addy turned to see a woman younger than her with a smile on her face. "He's a big hulk."

"I'll hulk you, woman."

Addy laughed as he attacked her neck. "Senji, my Senji, stop and let me meet your family." She pointed a finger at him when he released her. She turned. "You must be Miki, I'm Addy, it's wonderful to meet you." Going forward she grabbed the girl's hands before hugging her. "I'm sorry, I'm a hugger."

"All's well Addy, a pleasure to meet my brothers' mate. I have waited so long for him to find you, my sister."

"My son!"

Addy jumped when the yell came to see a huge man walk toward them.

"Ah, dear, you must be Addison, the little Earth female who nailed Korth in the balls."

"By the Gods, Kolad. Must you be so crude? Hello dear, I'm, Aliana, Senji's mother."

Addy smiled. "Hello." She glanced back and smiled up at Senji when his hand settled onto her lower back.

"Mother, Father, my Addison."

Addy smiled and chatted with them as they entered a huge dining hall and noticed Bark there talking to another man.

"Bark. I should have known that's how you found out about Addison, Father." Senji stated as he stepped forward.

Addy noticed his tension and patted his arm as a man approached.

"Takios."

"Brother, I hear congratulations are in order."

Addy noticed how Senji nodded.

"This is Addison, my mate. Addison, my brother Takios."

Moving her gaze to his brother, she smiled. "It's wonderful to meet you Takios and Bark, don't you have someplace to be?"

Bark laughed. "Nope, I'm family sunshine. Watch her right hook, Takios, and do not piss her off."

Addy's lip lifted as she scoffed and punched his arm. "What are you saying, Barkolth?"

"Oh shit. She used my full name. I'm out."

"You dweeb." Addy felt Senji tense when a female asked what the festivities were about and glanced up at him as his eyes hardened and Bark stopped and stayed close.

"Oh, Senji, you're back. How wonderful."

Addy's gaze narrowed slightly. She knew women like her. "Well, hello," she smiled. "You must be Takios' companion. I'm Addison, Senji's mate. It's so nice to meet you, and listen to nothing Bark says. He's full of hot air." She grinned, noticing Senji's brow lift and Bark belt out a 'no I'm not'.

"Mate." Ekene yelped. "Since when?"

"Since we signed as mates, Ekene." Senji stated.

"You go away for hunting and find a mate, how the hell did you do that Senji?"

Addy's brow lifted at the venom in her tone. "I kind of dropped onto his lap," she chuckled. "After I punched Gion and broke his nose." Her nose crinkled and shoulders lifted with her smile. "Best ending of a fight ever." She turned her head when his father called for the meal to start. "Oh, good, I'm starving. Taking Senji's hand she motioned him to follow her. "Come on you guys, my belly's growling." Grabbing Bark's on the way by him, she led them both to the table and sat between them. Senji sat close to his fathers left and his brother to Kolad's right.

Glancing down, she smiled at Miki. She was a beautiful young woman, while she and Senji took after their father with their dark looks, Takios resembled their mom with lighter hair.

"I am not understanding all of these festivities just because Senji took a mate. No one did so when I became Takios' companion."

Addy shifted slightly to see Senji's jaw clench again.

"Ekene." Kolad said.

Addy glanced over at his father who had the same look as his youngest son.

"One of my children has found their mate by the signs of the Gods. For this there is much celebration. If you choose not to participate, you may leave."

Lowering her hand to Senji's thigh, she rubbed him slightly, his hand laying upon hers, gripping it gently. She knew he was mad and didn't blame him. This woman was a real peach. Leaning to him, she whispered. "I think I'd like to go, please," as Ekene argued with Takios.

Senji turned and met her gaze.

"I don't want to be near her negativity anymore." She lowered her gaze, then lifted her eyes to him again. He nodded sharply, his chair legs scratched as he rose and held his hand to her. Addy set her fingers upon his palm, the silence echoing in her ears as Bark rose as well and met Aliana and Kolad's gaze before finding Ekene's. "You are a very negative person. Maybe you got up on the wrong side of the bed this morning, but I highly doubt it. I do know one thing and I'm sorry

Takios, but her jealousy and selfishness exude from her very being and that is something I choose not to be around." Moving her gaze back to Senji, she followed as he led her out.

Addy shook when they hit the doorstep. "I am so sorry Senji, but I could not sit there with her anymore. I hope your parents don't hate me."

"My parents are aware of Ekene and her issues."

"She is so jealous. My God, I've never seen a woman with her eyes so intent on another man while hers is sitting right next to her. She has problems, and I can't be held accountable if she tries her shit with you or me."

Senji chuckled and lifted her against him. "My little one, I will not stop you-from one of your-rants-on her."

Bark hooted. "Damn, I want to be present for that if it happens."

Addy wrapped her arms around his neck and legs around his waist. "She just better keep her ass away from my man."

"Your man is taking you to his dwelling to make you orgasm all night." Senji grinned.

"Oh, is that even possible?"

"Let's find out."

"Ah, I'm out here, I need to find my mate, you two are too much for mere men." Bark stated.

CHAPTER 14

ADDY SMILED AS SHE moved to straddle his lap as he sat cross-legged on the bed. Her fingers threaded through his long hair as she lowered her mouth to his. "Do we have to get out of bed today?"

"No, but my family will most likely be calling soon."

"As long as Ekene does not come."

"She will not."

"Mmmm, how long do we have before they start showing up?" Her lips brushed his softly.

"After the midday meal."

"Oh good."

Senji chuckled. "My sweet, you are so passionate."

Addy lifted her head and met his gaze. "Only with you, my Senji." His irises grew and she attacked his mouth when his eyes glowed. They glowed for her and her alone and that was the best aphrodisiac she ever could have asked for. Her hands gripped his hair as he thrust up into her heat. They both sighed at the intense feeling of being with one another. "Oh, what you do to me." She breathed against the side of his head and clenched her Kegels around his thickness his groan released tingles from the back of her head to her spine.

Senji leaned forward, one hand at her back, the other on the bed keeping them up as he thrust into her.

"*Oh*, I, I like this."

Chuckling, he captured her mouth, then moved to under her chin, kissing, sucking, biting. She'd stated that several times to him last eve with different positions, one, she taught him. Laying her down on the bed, her legs over his thighs, he loomed above her, and thrust in, loving how her eyes glazed with the passion she had for him.

He lowered his head and sucked on her right nipple, until she lifted his head, moaning as they kissed. She tightened her Kegels on him, their chests heaving as he buried his face in her hair and thrust quickly, over and over again.

Addy cried out, her fingers clenching his shoulders, her pelvis jerked to meet his thrusts, his hand slid across her slick stomach down to her clit and she gasped, holding her breath, her heartbeat pounded in her throat as lightning flew through her. "Senji!"

"Release with me, sweet." He groaned as her muscles spasmed and thrust harder, faster, his cock hitting her womb and she moaned as she soared over the edge. Senji groaned as tingles ran from the back of his head, down his spine, directly to his dick and pushed forward as he burst inside her with a roar. His body shook as he lay his cheek next to hers, his hips arching once more as the last of his essence entered her warmth. Shifting to her left, he lay down, her hand on his chest until their breathing evened out.

"Dang Senji, I never want to leave this bed." Turning, she smiled at him, her hand cupping the side of his face.

"Then you will miss out on all the other areas in my dwelling I plan to give you an orgasm on."

*

Addy smiled as she watched Senji with his siblings. It seemed when Takios was not around Ekene, he was very pleasant and there was no tension.

"You see it as well, don't you?" Aliana asked.

"If you mean no Ekene, no tension, yes. Senji didn't tell me a lot about her. He wanted me to make up my own mind. Except for one thing."

"Ah, he told you she approached him for sex."

Addy whipped her head to her right, eyes wide as she met her mother-in-law's gaze. "You know about that?"

Aliana smiled. "Oh yes, Miki overheard the whole incident, although Senji does not know this."

Her gaze ran over the woman in front of her. "Does Takios know?"

"Yes. When Senji left with no warning to go hunting, he couldn't figure out why and Miki let us all know, without Ekene's presence of course."

"And how did he take it?"

"Not well at first, he was in denial, but he knows his brother, and knows Senji would never do anything to hurt him. Then a number of our warriors—with whom she had also attempted to mate—came forward.

Addy shook her head. "I'm sorry, what?"

"Oh yes, she is quite the..."

"Whore."

Aliana chuckled. "Yes."

"Why hasn't Takios sent her packing?"

"If you mean, send her home. He wanted to do his own research and right before Senji and you arrived at our dwelling, he received all his answers."

Addy glanced out at the three siblings, the two brothers teasing Miki. They were so close. "I've never had brothers or sisters. In fact, I don't even know who my parents were. I was given up for adoption. My grandmother found me when I was eighteen and we got to know each other. I've never had such a bond with someone, other than Senji. I can't even imagine what those three have gone through emotionally because of Ekene. I do know the intense emotions at being ripped from Senji when Korth attacked, and that's something I never want to go through again."

She glanced up when Aliana's hand touched her shoulder.

"What do you mean, Korth attacked and took you from Senji?"

"Oh, it's been taken care of. He let me go after a few hours..."

"Yeah," Bark chuckled. "After she beat the crap out of his men and talked her way back to Senji."

"Shut up, Bark."

"Oh, hell's fires, no. Aunt Aliana, you should know who Senji mated to. This little Cion Three female here..."

Bark chuckled, stepping away as Addy went to hit him. "Get over here, mouth."

"Oh, I'm the mouth? Don't piss her off, Auntie."

"Senji!" Addy grinned as her man stopped and looked her way. "Tell Bark to stop messing with me before he pisses me off."

"Damn it, Bark. Can you not behave?" Senji called out.

"No!" Bark laughed as he moved to them.

Addy grinned as Senji's long black hair swirled as he went to punch Bark on the arm and Takios joined in. Miki jumped in and Addison laughed, lifting her hands to cover her lips.

"Addison."

Addy lowered her hands as she met Aliana's gaze.

"You are the only female I have ever seen make him this happy. The Gods have blessed you both."

"I have never been happier. I know we'll have arguments and stuff. Well, we already have, but I will never do anything to hurt him Aliana. He has my heart." She glanced down when tears gathered. She looked over at Senji quickly before meeting her gaze again. "I haven't even told him that yet. I told him I loved him, but, not that he has my heart."

CHAPTER 15

SENJI SIGHED AS HIS head went back, enjoying the heated water of the large bathing pool and grinned, turning to meet her gaze. "Why are you staring so?"

"There's something I have to tell you."

"What's that, my sweet?" He drew her to straddle his lap, enjoying the feel of her bare skin caressing his.

Addy caressed the side of his face, then cupped both sides. "You have my heart, Senji Ootook."

His head tilted, his gaze on her. "As you have mine, my Addison." Leaning forward, he brushed his lips gently across hers as her hands caressed his shoulders.

"Ooh, wait." Addy drew back, jumping from the pool.

"Ah, we're kissing here." Admiring the view of her naked backside.

"I have something for you. I bought it today at the market with your mom and sister."

"And that's more important than kissing on me and getting to feel you up?"

"Just hold on."

Senji leaned back in the water with his hands behind his head and reclined back in the pool, and grinned when hands caressed him. "Well, that didn't take long. Get back in here."

"Certainly."

His eyes popped open. "What are you doing here?" he snarled, turning to face his brother's companion.

Ekene smiled. "Getting my visit in. Everyone left me at the dwelling today."

"With good right!"

"Do you know how hard it is to sneak out of your parents dwelling without being seen and then to have to hide in the shadows until your little, whatever she is finally left you alone?"

Get out of my dwelling!"

"Now Senji, don't be like that." Ekene grinned. "You know you missed me."

Senji moved away from the edge of the pool. "Hell fires, get out!"

"Quiet now, you wouldn't want your little-mate to come back too quickly."

"She's back." Addy stated as she stepped out of the shadows. "I suggest you get the fuck away from my man."

Ekene smiled. "Don't you know he invited me?"

"I did no such thing!" Senji bellowed, grabbing a towel and wrapped it around Addy as he stepped out.

"Oh, I know." Addy replied, stepping in front of Senji when Ekene's gaze went down. "I suggest you do as my mate says and leave."

Senji glanced down at Addy as he wrapped a towel around his waist. He had never heard her tone so low or shit, lethal. His eyes widened when she pulled a short sword and stepped toward Ekene, sending her screaming and running out. "Computer get me a link to Takios now." He stated as he headed toward his clothing center.

"Hey what's up?"

"Ekene just ran from my dwelling, she tried to assert herself again and Addison didn't take kindly to it."

"What? By the hell fires what's she up to now?"

"I don't know brother, but..." Senji turned around his gaze taking in the room.

"Don't know what?"

"Hold on. Addison?" he called out quickly scanning his bedchamber, running to the door he flung it open. "Addison!" Going by the window, he noticed his cruiser gone and ran to her clothing center to see her gear from when they trapped the Suknan gone. "Shit."

"What the hell is happening?"

"Addison's gone after Ekene. Wake up the guard, she's not going to be easy to stop. She's geared up. I'll call Bark." He grabbed his shirt. "Link end."

*

Addy knew Ekene stayed at Senji's parents dwelling, as Takios resided in one of the large living wings. Her hand fisted as the computer stated they were arriving, and she jumped out, her gaze on Ekene as she ran up the stairs. Grabbing the hair band, she tied back her hair in a ponytail as she strode forward. Stepping into the main hall her gaze narrowed. "You and I have unfinished business."

"What, no!"

"Oh yes." Taking a step as Ekene backed up, she noticed men running in from the side.

"Takios, stop her, she's crazy!"

"Senji has informed me of what happened. She has every right to deal with you, Ekene." Takios stated. "You went into their dwelling and made advancements to her mate, my brother!"

Addy moved forward; she knew it wouldn't take Senji long to realize she was gone. Her nostrils flared as the female argued with him, her anger rising as she insisted Senji told her to meet him. "You lie!" Running, she lowered her left shoulder and body slammed right into her, sending her flying. Skidding, she went after her, lifting her up. "You have lied for the last time on this matter and the last time you will make advances to my mate!" She dodged to the left when Ekene struck out, and came up with a right hook, catching Ekene on the side of the head. Turning quickly, Addy grabbed her hair, head-butting her and knew she broke her nose before tossing Ekene with force to the other side of the room. "Get up!"

"No, no more."

Addy strode to her as she scrambled to her feet. "Get up, you bitch!"

"Addison." Her ears perked with his low tone, hand fisted as she stared at the woman in front of her. Glancing to her right, she met Senji's gaze.

"She's not a fighter, and you have drawn blood. Call it done."

"I'm still pissed."

"Yes."

"I'm still pissed!" Her hand fisted and she punched her thigh. "She came into our home and hit on you! Then tried to blame you!"

"Yes, and you have dealt with it."

"I want to beat her to a bloody damn pulp." Her chest heaved, fingers on her left hand strumming her thigh as her right one clenched. Nostrils flared as she closed her eyes, her breasts rising with the deep breath.

"Takios will deal with her now."

He was right behind her, calming but knowing not to touch her as she came down. Her eyelids fluttered to see two guards taking Ekene by the arms and stepped forward. "If you ever come near me or my Senji again. I will kill you." Her gaze narrowed as Ekene's gaze widened, and she whimpered as they dragged her from the hall. Taking a breath and a moment before she turned to meet his gaze.

"You took off on me."

"Yep."

"How did you get the cruiser to follow your command?"

"I told it to."

"You, my sweet, have an uncanny knack for working around items that should stop you."

"I can't help it." When Senji smiled, she tilted her head. "I think I hurt my hand."

"Most likely."

Her ears perked with a cough and an 'I told you so', gaze narrowing, and lips pursed. "Shut up Bark."

"What?" Bark chuckled. "I told everyone here, you're a force to be reckoned with when you're pissed."

Addy glanced around at all the people in the hall. Not only the family, but guards and servants. Her gaze quickly meeting Senji's. "I'm sorry, I didn't mean to embarrass you."

Senji grinned. "You have not. Now let's go to the med center."

"Way to show her, my sister." Miki smiled.

Addy shyly leaned into Senji as they walked by his parents. "I apologize for disturbing your household." She liked how his arm went over her shoulders.

"You took care of business." Aliana stated.

"I knew I liked you." Kolad chuckled. "Good to know my son has a strong mate, when needed."

Addy nodded and went quietly with Senji, letting the medical team heal her hands and check her over for any other hurts.

"Are you all right?"

"I am. I just do not like that side of myself." Lifting her gaze when he stepped between her legs, his hands cupped her face and tilting it up until she met his eyes.

"We all have that side Addison, some worse than others. I've only ever seen you act like way when we're in danger, or when you nailed that Suknan, but he was bound for more. The positive side is you know when to stop."

"I didn't want to stop tonight. I think-I think, I really would have killed her if you hadn't stopped me."

"And you trusted me when I asked you to stop. You trusted my word."

"It took me a few moments to get under control."

"That is normal. No one can switch on or off that quickly. You are an honorable female, and I am happy to have you for my mate."

The sides of her mouth lifted with a soft smile. "And I am honored to be your mate my Senji."

Senji wiggled his brows. "Good, now let's get back to our dwelling. We have unfinished business as well."

"Oh, *oh*." Addy lifted her hand, taking the band out and presented it to him. "This is what I was going to get for you. I saw it in the market and thought it would look nice in your hair." Her eyes were on him as he lowered his and picked up the hair band made with brown and gold forvine, a gem on his planet, and smiled when he did. "It reminded me of your eyes, especially when they glow for me."

Senji lifted the hair band from her hand and drew his back with it. "It is perfect my sweet, thank you."

Addy smiled as she leaned forward, kissing him. "I love you, my Senji."

"As I love you, my Addison."

Addy signed as he drew her into his arms and met his kiss. It was soft and sensual.

"Ah, there's my little ass kicker." Bark said as he entered. "How you feeling, Addy? All healed up?"

"Yes, thank you."

"Don't you have someplace to be?" Senji asked.

Addy giggled when Bark replied *nope*. "I think we need to find him a mate."

Senji grinned as she met his gaze. "I believe you are right."

The End

Excerpt from **SPACE WARRIOR**

Releasing: **April 6th, 2024**

"Father, what are those?" Malia asked, pointing to the two silver objects streaming through the sky.

"Those are Space Warriors. They come and take the bad ones away. Now lift your mask. The winds are picking up."

Malia rubbed her palm over her face, brushing her hair back. She hadn't thought of her father in years. Maybe coming back to Scurn III wasn't a great idea. "One more stop and then I'm gone," Malia muttered as she slung back her drink. Rising, she tossed a few credits on the counter, lifted her mask, and headed out into the windy afternoon.

Everyone in the system referred to the four planets around the giant star as the Desolate Expanse. Malia called them home. Unless you were born on one of them, you didn't stay. Hell, she didn't know why she came back, but as long as she was here, there was one person she would see.

*

"You should not have come."

Malia met the old woman's eye. "You're the only one I have left, my only family."

"Yes, but do you not listen to your guides? Malia," she sighed, shaking her head. "Coming back will be your death."

Malia's chin lowered to touch her chest. "Then it is my death. I am so tired, Aunt Tula. I cannot do this anymore."

"Tired means you are alive."

Malia followed her outside into the sunshine to the edge of the cliff.

"You came on the wrong day, Malia, but I suppose it is fate, as a family member should be present."

A twisting streaked through her stomach. "Present for what?"

"It's my time, Malia. Listen to your guides. They will keep you alive."

The crushed rock crunched beneath her boots as Malia ran for the edge, her hand skimming the material of her aunt's dress. "No!" Reaching down, she missed again. Wide- eyed, Tula smiled at her before closing her eyes. Her chest ached, heaving sobs and sounds Malia hadn't heard since her father passed. Fingers clenched the crushed rock and dirt beneath, her aunt gone from her sight. Now she was truly alone.

"Malia Bash'ar, I'm Commander Ruskin. You are charged with murder, smuggling, and theft according to the laws of the Scorpii galaxy. You will come with me to stand trial for these charges."

Malia turned her head enough to see him from the corner of her eye. "Go away, Space Warrior." Her words choked, wet trails through the dust covering her face.

"I will not repeat myself. You are tagged as armed and dangerous. I will shoot to kill."

Malia chuckled through her misery, sharp edges of the crushed stone biting into her flesh. "Good! Because I have nothing left!" Rising, she turned, her gaze meeting the reflective helmet he wore. Head turned slightly; her eyes closed as the hot wind blew over her. "Nothing." Her whispered words barely met his ears as she stepped back. "Let me make it easy for you, Space Warrior. All you have to do is bring my genetic material back." Malia pushed off the edge of the cliff, her arms going out as the wind rushed her back, neck-length hair flying up around her face. She could already feel the change in the air, the depleted oxygen as she plummeted down. The good thing about her planet was the intense drops in breathable air. She'd black out before she hit bottom.

Malia's eyes drifted open when her body jerked.

"Not today Malia Bash'ar," Ruskin said as he caught her.

"I did not, do it." Malia whispered before blackness ensued.

UNDERCOVER LOVER SERIES
ZACK

GABE

JAKE

MITCH - Prequel

Being part of a special police unit, love was the last emotion these four brothers thought they would have to deal with.

Until they ran into the women who yanked their heartstrings.

GALACTIC FEDERATION SERIES:
Sub-series: RETREIVERS
LOVING JANESKA
SEDUCING SOMA
MELLA

They are Retrievers. If something is stolen, they are hired to get it back.

They go in unseen and unnoticed, however getting out without being shot at, is another story. They are one of the best teams in the Federation and are paid handsomely for their services.

They are family.

<u>DESTINED TO MATE</u>

A feline mated to a werewolf?
As a Chimera, half lioness/half human, Alexis Xanthis, has never released the beast within. Until she meets Lykan Alpha, Morgan LeVey. Being near him triggers a powerful need to mate, but is Morgan strong enough to dominate her feline side and still handle the human half with a gentle hand? And will the powers that be allow it?

Authors Note

Thank you for taking the time to read,
Addison & The Bounty Hunter.
Space Warrior and The Dragon King & *The Shadow* of The Bounty
Hunter sub-series in The Galactic Federation Series, are coming next.
As always, read lots and stay spicy!

Love a book?
Help others find it by leaving a review.
Authors will love you for it!
Thanks!

A little bio

I have served as the Vice President of Communications and as Vice President of Programs for my former RWA chapter in Florida.

A Slave's Way Out, won The Torrid Title of the Year Award and made me a bestselling Author.

Writing is my passion and I look forward to it every day!

Not so much the editing, LOL. ☺

I bow to my editor! She has her work cut out for her. ☺

Where to Find me ...
www.AuthorCASalo.com[1]
Facebook: AuthorCASalo

Books2Read

Books2Read is my self-publishing platform and offers Amazon, Kobo, Apple, Smashwords, Indigo, Nook and more!

Amazon – Author Page

---

1. http://www.AuthorCASalo.com